Time Enough for Sadness

Tantalizing, quietly devasting fiction

John P. Asling

The Choir Press

First published in the United Kingdom in 2020 by
The Choir Press.

ISBN 978-1-78963-141-8

In Memory
of
Viola Asling (Godman)

'There'll be time enough for sadness when you leave me.'

KRIS KRISTOFFERSON

Contents

First Words

Voices in the wind.
Listen . . .
it takes a village –
to raise a child,
nurse a child,
nurture a child,
shape a child,
(Oh God) rape a child,
kill a child,
bury a child,
mourn a child.

Voices in the wind.
Listen . . .
it takes a village –
to create community,
tear community,
mend community,
liberate community,
grieve community,
unite community,
rebuild community.

Voices in the wind.
Listen . . .
You are not merely –
bricks.
mortar.
houses.
flats.
churches.
markets.
shops.
halls.

Voices in the wind.
Listen . . .
you are
people,
villagers,
in
community
living
through
seasons of your life.

A Time for Every Matter

This is Grace's moment.

Just step into the aisle. Make your way up to the front of the church. To the microphone standing erect beside that man framed in the colour photograph. That man perched on a pedestal. That man smiling down on the incense-shrouded congregation. That man dwarfed by the looming bare wooden cross.

It is the first moment of silence in the hour that has until now been filled with precious words sung by the royally garbed women's choir, tears of grief solemnly pronounced by the ageing minister before the grey suits, black dresses, bowed heads.

Words like 'hero', like 'courage'.

Clutching a scribbled note in her fingers with their blood-red painted nails, Grace turns toward the aisle. She's just one worshipper, a man, away from stepping from her usual seat in the back pew and she hesitates, hoping he will discreetly let her pass. In that moment, words from the Bible read by the dead man's brother echo in her soul.

'For everything there is a season, and a time for every matter under heaven.'

For everything? Every matter? There is no season for what he did to me. No season and no reason.

*

Everett and Grace were paired for the night at the homeless shelter in the basement of their church not far from the village centre. This was the first time they had worked so closely together, though she knew him from church. He talked to her a little about his children.

'Thanks for taking care of the girls. They love you looking after them. You're so good with them,' he said one Sunday.

She didn't offer much in reply, partly because she was shy, but she was also somehow wary. If someone had asked her, she wouldn't have been able to tell them why.

'It's okay, they're very well behaved, those girls.'

Everett and Grace worked side-by-side, blowing up mattresses, putting on the thin fitted sheets, threadbare blankets, bleached pillow slips. How uncomfortable those narrow beds looked crowded into that basement meeting room. But at least it was warm inside. Outside it was a bone-chilling January. Everett and Grace made a pot of tea and set it on the communal table and replenished the supply of broken biscuits donated by the factory. The men and women booked for the night – twenty-five in all – were hungry and thirsty when they first arrived at the village church from various parts of the London borough. Some of the 'guests' – the shelter leader insisted on calling them that – perused the box of used clothes Everett and Grace had set out, trying on woolly hats and jumpers.

Grace was always surprised they never looked like the homeless people she saw on the street near the station. They didn't look to be much worse off than her. And that scared her. Was this her next stop, now that she had been let go at the nail salon and her share of the rent was overdue? Everett had explained that the borough had 'screened' the people using their church shelter because it was run by volunteers. 'We do this out of our best Christian instincts, but of course we aren't trained.'

Everett and Grace warmed the lasagnes baked by the church ladies group, prepared the garlic bread the men made, set the tables, made the coffee and filled the water jugs. Then they took a break.

'The demographics are changing,' he said, adding milk to his mug of tea. And to hers. Grace just watched. He was well informed on the refugee situation because he is an elder and spoke often to the minister. Grace listened, blowing softly on her steaming tea.

The 'guests' were mostly Eastern Europeans and North Africans working in restaurants or doing day labour. One was a tall man with a thin moustache, who grew up not far from where Grace's father was born. Grace heard him talking to one of the locals who had got tired of sleeping in his car and had come to the shelter for the first time.

'I can't go back to my country,' the African man said. 'I'm a dead man if I go back there. No way I'm going back there. But

God, it's cold here now. I sure could use that hot sun on my back.'

The other man laughed for a moment, then caught himself. 'You'll be all right here. It'll come good. You wait and see.'

Grace was wiping tables nearby, but took in the exchange, especially the part about her father's country in Africa, but kept her thoughts to herself.

Two volunteers were missing from the overnight roster and Grace said she would stay on, not having to get up for work in the morning. She'd get breakfast, cut down on expenses, every little bit helps. She was thinking that way more and more since losing her job.

Everett said he was available too.

'Keep the team together.' He laughed easily but his eyes were stern. Grace had noticed that, over the years since Everett joined the church from the other side of the city. She knew him from his greetings at the church door, his speeches at meetings and the time he had preached on 'charity' when the pastor was on leave. Some Sunday mornings she worked in the nursery where his two youngsters were an island of serenity in an ocean of manic children.

Grace wondered why Everett wouldn't want to get home to his wife and two small girls with bows in their hair. Last week, Grace had looked after them again in the church nursery. They had played together with Barbie dolls and the carers didn't need to fuss over them. She guessed Everett just wanted to help out. He had that kind of reputation at the church. A good Christian man.

It was a long night at the shelter. The aroma of the vegetarian lasagne eventually gave way to the stench of men's feet, along with other body odours. The three women in their curtained-off corner had quietened down. Just before lights out, an older man with shaking hands began cursing at the youngster next to him for shifting his mattress too close. Everett went to calm them. The shift leader had to step between the two young labourers wearing coloured baseball caps trying to use the same plug for their phones. Grace finished cleaning the kitchen like she always did. Things quietened down by midnight.

Grace looked through her emails on her smartphone, then closed her eyes, just resting. Everett read a book in the dimly lit hallway. The shift leader read her Bible by the stove light in the kitchen.

In the morning Everett offered to drive Grace home. She usually walked but agreed when the shock of frigid air hit her as they left the shelter at six o'clock. Frost enveloped Everett's sleek red car but it started immediately. He reached very carefully across her to help with the tangled seat belt.

'There, that's better, Grace. The children get them messed up,' he laughed. Those eyes. Grace nodded, thinking of the pretty bows and the Barbie dolls.

'Those girls are lovely,' she offered, too tired for much talk. Closed her eyes.

'The joy of my life,' he responded. 'They love it when you take care of them.'

They drove in silence towards Grace's cramped flat on the other side of the village, but Everett suddenly steered the humming red sports car down an alley, stopped abruptly, and locked the doors. Grace couldn't breathe. Her mouth went dry. She couldn't speak. This time Everett's reach was sudden, brutal. She smelled his foul breath as he tore at her jeans, her T-shirt, ripped them off her, forced himself onto her, into her. She tried to bite his neck but couldn't get a hold, gritted her teeth, managing to spit out one word: 'No.'

He was deaf to her. Grace thought she would vomit – the touch of him, the sound of him, the rocking of the car. Grace thought she would die; wished she had died.

*

Back in her flat, Grace let the hot water of the shower mix with her tears. She stayed under for a long time, thinking. *I am just a piece of dead meat. Because of that man. Everett. He has eaten me up, tossed me aside like a carcass.* She tried to pray but felt that somehow God had died when that man, that Everett, forced himself on her.

'Where is the pastor's loving God now?' Grace wailed then collapsed onto her bed, falling into a morbid sleep.

She stayed in her bed for hours, ignoring her buzzing phone, not eating, not answering the door, not caring about anything, anybody. Like she was dying. *That man, that Everett, he did this. Raped me.*

She couldn't move from under the blankets on her sweat-drenched bed for days, slept, wept.

Then suddenly one morning she got up, pulled her curtains open, saying, 'Fuck him. I'm not letting him kill me. Hell no.'

*

'It's not your fault just because you got in that posh car with that Everett,' Grace's friend Franny fumed a week later. 'You've got to say something. You've got to go to the police. You've got to tell. Got to go tell it. The whole story.'

Grace knew Franny never trusted Everett, his young wife, perfect kids. She'd say, 'What's the matter with women his own age? There's something about that man, Grace. You see it too. I know you do.'

Grace had never responded to Franny's questions.

*

Early one Saturday morning, a few weeks later, Franny sent Grace a text saying Everett had been stabbed to death. Grace dropped her phone on to the kitchen table, couldn't look at it. Then she picked it up, read the message again. *How is this possible? What happened?*

She went online and read about it herself, sitting up in her frigid flat as the groan of morning traffic started growing on the village high street below. 'Jesus,' she whispered. 'That man, that Everett. Dead.'

A 45-year-old man was stabbed to death early this morning as he attempted to stop a knifing outside an after-hours club. Everett Winston, a broker, was pronounced dead at University Hospital at 4 a.m. A Met spokesman said the investigation was ongoing. However, one woman, who refused to give her name, hailed Mr Winston as a 'hero'. 'He put his body on the line, took a blade.' The Met said while they were still gathering information, it appears the slain man's 'courage' prevented major bloodshed. Mr Winston leaves a wife and twin three-year-old daughters.

Franny phoned Grace a few minutes later. 'Hero? What's that Everett doing down there at that hour? I'm sorry about those two little kids but what's that man doing there at that hour with all those youngsters?'

'Looks like he was some kind of hero, Franny.'

'You know better than that, Grace. It's like that Hollywood guy. They're never who they say they are.'

'Maybe none of us are, Franny.'

'Don't talk shit to me.'

'I just don't know.'

*

The bloke in her row looks over at Grace like he knows what's on her mind. Was he Everett's friend? There's nobody at the 'open mic' and the minister is asking if anyone else has anything to add about 'Our dear friend Everett, who laid down his life for others'. There's been plenty of folks talking about all the good things Everett had done at the church, leading that building committee last year, organizing the fundraiser for Syria. Grace makes herself skinny as possible, so she won't be touching the man beside her as she moves past him and closer to the aisle. He doesn't move but Grace gets by. The minister is talking about what the newspapers have been saying about Everett, but Grace hears more of the words uttered by Everett's brother.

'A time to be born and a time to die.'

When's my time to be born, my time to live?

*

Grace never told Franny about the envelope. Franny would have shrieked, like the time her father screamed at her for smoking weed. Sometimes she's loud about protecting her rights. That's just not Grace's way.

She had stopped helping at the shelter after Everett

attacked her. She told the shelter leader she needed to spend more time looking for work after losing her job. Grace had done Franny's nails and then Franny flashed her silver-sparkled fingers at their friends at the nearby mall and told them Grace needed business. Grace set up shop in the tiny kitchen of the flat she shared with her mum and a few of the girls came over the next week and got their nails painted. She charged them a few quid, helped her get groceries. But she knew she had to find another job. Something more secure. She wanted to save money to go to college.

Then the envelope arrived. Grace opened and read the message on a plain card.

Sorry for what happened the other night. I possibly misread the situation. Hope this ends the matter.

'This' was £100 in twenties. Grace looked at it spread out like a fan as it fell from the envelope. *Misread? Fuck. The matter? The rape.*

She took the envelope to church next Sunday, sat in the back row, eyeing Everett and his pretty wife in their usual pew. When the elders came for the Offering she put the envelope containing the £100 in the basket. The note was in there too.

After church, Grace met Franny for coffee at the cheap café beside the station. They sat in the back booth as usual. Franny grabbed her best friend's hand across the table.

'You gone to the police yet? Grace, you can't keep this all to yourself.'

Grace took a sip of her coffee, dabbed her unpainted lips with the napkin.

'No police, Franny. I got other plans. Maybe I forgive him.'
'Well, maybe I'm going talk to his pretty wife, then.'
'No, you aren't.'
'Yes, I am.'
'No, Franny, this is my battle.'
'Hope you know what you're doing, Gracie.'
'Me too.'

That was before Everett became a hero.

Grace thinks the minister is going to close down that open mic before she gets to the front of the church. Grace moves toward the solitary microphone, thinks again about the passage from the Bible read by Everett's brother.

'A time to mourn and a time to dance.'

I'm not mourning, and I am not dancing. I am moving up there.

*

After coffee in the café, Grace ignored Franny's phone calls for a few days. She didn't tell her about the envelope, and she didn't tell her about going to the 'Memorial for a Hero' at the church. Franny's folks would be there, so she would know about it, but Franny mostly did the opposite of whatever they said. She stayed out late, refused to go to church. Grace used to be like that. Since her mum and dad divorced, after her mum had an affair with that Warner, she had had no energy for protesting, stirring things up. Except now there was Everett. The rape. *Fuck him. What's he done to me? What am I going to do about it?*

Grace dressed for church like it was Sunday, sat down at her kitchen table and took out her notepad, ripped out a few sheets and started scratching out all the words that had been bouncing around inside her head. Her whole body shook like she was on some fairground ride. When she was finished, she put the pen down, wiped her eyes dry, put the note in her bag and headed out the door to church.

*

Grace's short legs are moving quickly as she approaches the front of the church. She is almost there. The minister doesn't want her up here. His almighty glare is telling her that. The choir of sweet-scented ladies are glaring down at her. The big cross up front is judging her. She hears those words again: 'hero' and 'courage' but can't fit them alongside Everett's words: 'Keep the team together', 'misread the situation'. She can see the fan of twenties on her kitchen table. Once more, Grace hears the words of the Bible passage read by Everett's brother.

'A time to keep silence and a time to speak.'
Grace's time of silence is over.
She steps up to the microphone, takes a deep breath.
'The Good Book says ...'

Never Right

'Is he alright?' the father asks.

He never has been, the mother thinks. Never right.

The father glances down at the infant wrapped in blue, resting between them. He pulls his scarf up to keep out the wind, which is from the north again and bitter in the late-afternoon sunshine.

'Course he is,' she responds, her words clipped like bullet points in a briefing paper.

'As well as can be expected,' he adds.

'Yes. Of. Course.'

It's been their favourite bench, gnarled old wooden planks and scuffed black iron frame, with a plaque honouring people called Henry and Jane Gooding, who met and fell in love on this spot overlooking the Maritime Museum many years ago. How quaint, she has often thought.

He likes the bench and the view, though he longs to travel on rivers more exotic than this.

She's always been too busy at her government job. Day and night.

It has been their meeting place, not for romantic reasons, but for more mundane ones. This is where they have always come to make their most difficult decisions. They bought the house near the heath after talking it through on this bench. They used to talk much more. Then there was the abortion when their first child was found to be damaged in utero; the second child was also not normal, so there was another weighty conversation, then another abortion.

They decided to keep the third, a surprise – this disfigured boy, one they were told would never live a normal life. A gift or a dilemma? It depended on which expert they consulted. The father had his suspicions but didn't really know for certain.

And now this latest decision – her decision. The father was too weak to fight her off. She had too much on him. When he lost his first antique shop in Blackheath after months of fiddling the books, she rescued him, helped set him up again in Greenwich, took charge, and threatened to turn him over to the tax people, if ever he got out of line.

Now it's time to act, but she wants to ask if the hole he dug a few days ago in the thick wooded garden twenty yards away is deep enough. He had complained about how hard the ground would be in the middle of winter, but it had been mild and damp for a week. She made sure that the timing was right. That's what she's good at. He'd better have got his part right. He is often weak on details. Always weak. She understands this is the way he is in terms of maintenance around the house, the MOT for the car. But this is different. It has to be done right.

He wonders if the blanket is warm enough, though he dares not ask. He thinks she will forget her vow of silence and lash out one more time at his weakness. What does it matter now? It's too late for caring. He hugs himself to warm himself against the wind.

She glares at him from the corner of her eye.

Then the infant opens its eyes, begins to cry loudly.

The father immediately reaches toward the child, but the mother issues a low moaning 'Noooooo' from her rigid mouth and the father pulls his hand away.

So, they sit stiff as strangers while the infant wails for the longest time. There are few passers-by on this cold Monday afternoon, though one old man in a sailor's jacket and cap stares at them momentarily before limping down the nearby path, marking each step of the way with his oak walking stick. Click. Click. Click.

Soon the infant stops crying, though it still seems to be shivering beneath the blanket.

Mother and father are silent, watching a police boat seemingly chase a tourist vessel up the river toward St. Paul's Cathedral.

She remembers the time they went to church, tried to talk to the vicar about the impending birth, about the complications, the difficulties. The vicar looked like the fellow who played a Roman Catholic priest on that television special filmed up in Liverpool, a broken soul with a face wrinkled with understanding. But there was no Jimmy McGovern writing his script. The real-life vicar was all Bible and bile. No empathy. So, they fled.

The wind whips around them as the sun sets. There is no one else in the park.

'It's almost dark enough,' she says.

'Don't do this. I refuse . . .'

She shakes her head. 'Shut up. You lost that right a long time ago.'

He begins to weep.

So weak, she thinks.

'I'll do it,' she says.

'No,' he responds.

But he is too late. Far too late.

She is on her feet. She picks up the bundle and disappears deep into the brush.

He is fixed to the bench, unable to move, eyes closed.

*

It isn't Rake's first day on the job, but it feels like it. The well-travelled redheaded detective hasn't dressed right for the spring's dampness or the wind blowing at the top of the hill overlooking the misty Thames. To top it off, he's been partnered with the toff Terrance Prentice-Jones – 'Pinstripe' – those bloody suits, magnets for office secretaries. This, after Rake has been off for six months for what they used to call 'nerves' when he started at the Met thirty years ago, but which Human Resources now refers to as 'mental health' issues. Wonder what Pinstripe's heard? That his wife left him? Probably. About the months of IVF, the miscarriages? Possibly. That was between him and the Met chaplain. But word gets out. The force is a sieve. No matter.

But that bloody wind makes him shiver.

Rake sits down at the gnarly old bench yards from where forensics are doing their morbid business. It's too soon to approach, and he's not anxious to do so from the little he's heard about the case so far. Though he hopes he's heard wrong. *A child? Buried in the bush?* Rake needs time to figure out how to face this case, and make sure no one can read his mind on it.

Pinstripe approaches.

'Back from holidays then, are you, David?'

He sits beside Rake, too close, looking towards the Thames.

Pinstripe is the only detective at the Greenwich station that calls him that. To everyone else, it's Rake.

'Had enough of the sun in Corfu, thought I'd make sure you didn't screw this up.'

Rake isn't prepared to take any shit on his first day back. Not from Pinstripe, or anyone else for that matter.

'Let's get to it, then,' Pinstripe says.

Rake figures that Pinstripe knows what's been happening with him, knows enough about him to back off a bit too, at least for the time being. Rake's got rep as a snarly bugger. He smiles at that. He's a good cop. He know that's also part of his reputation on the force. Pinstripe won't mind working alongside of him. However, Rake will keep an eye on him.

Rake leads the way across the twenty yards of damp grass to where the yellow tent covers the deep brush garden area. Pinstripe, almost a foot taller than Rake, gets there first and lifts the tape so Rake can cross the line. As they get close to where the uniform guards the scene, they glance at one another.

'It's a baby. Fucking shame.'

It's a woman's voice, coming from behind them. Rake turns to face the coroner, Dr Michaelson. She is well dressed, smart and takes no guff from detectives. Rake is happy to see her, happier still to turn away from the body.

'What can you tell us?' Rake ventures. He knows not to press this woman too hard or she clams up.

Pinstripe looks like he wants to add something but bites his tongue.

'Just this,' Michaelson says. 'This isn't any ordinary baby. And this isn't any ordinary death.'

'Is it murder?' Pinstripe pitches.

'I've never seen a case like this before and I bet neither of you have either.'

She starts to say more, stops herself.

'What the hell?' Rake says, shaking his head. The rumours were true. *Baby*, he thinks, trying to get his breath, trying to remember what the chaplain had counselled for dealing with cases like this. *But, a baby?* He wipes his eyes with his sleeve, says no more.

Pinstripe grimaces. 'Come on, doc, what are you talking about?'

There is a long silence. At least there are no words, though the wind continues to whistle around them. Rake is shivering now. Pinstripe brushes at his damp jacket.

'You fellows follow politics?' Michaelson asks.

*

They sit on the bench staring straight ahead, not talking. He is well dressed as usual, a pale blue three-piece suit garnished with a pink tie. Over-dressed even in early summer, she thinks. Some things don't change. She inhales that cheap scent, a habit adopted before his success in business, before politics, before the Cabinet. He is more thickset than her husband, yet still handsome, confident. That's what she once admired. At this moment, she is annoyed at his playing with the ring on his left little finger. And unforgiving of herself for seeing him one last time a year ago, long after the end of the affair.

A night to remember, he had promised her. She wouldn't forget it. He drank too much. She drank too much – spirits, which she should never touch. It's not that he forced her. She would never say that. But he had a kind of brute force – in the office and in the bedroom. He always got what he wanted.

We'll see, she thinks.

He looks flushed, probably can feel his heart pulsing through his whole body. Probably wants to ask her how the fuck this happened. Probably can barely contain himself. Definitely wants a cigarette but doesn't want her to know. But she knows him all too well. She looks over at him. He can barely get his breath, reaches into his pocket for a pill. He glances at his driver, twenty yards away, leaning against a willow, checking his watch.

'Burying the child! Tying a note to the child! What the fuck was that? This will ruin me – and you! This could bring down the fucking government! We haven't got the numbers! You know this business. You put it all at risk! I could have sorted this.'

'Like you sorted your marriage so we could have a new start?'

They both stare straight ahead, refuse to look at each other.

'Have you noticed that driver over there? He's about to take me to Number 10 for a meeting with the Prime Minister. For fuck's sake. I'm going cap in bloody hand. I'm not sure this mess can be sorted. I've held off the press with a few trinkets for now, but you know what they're like. You've overplayed your hand. The child! What in God's name were you thinking?'

'It was sick.'

'Sick?'

'You know what I mean.'

'Challenged, they say now. It's not a death sentence – it shouldn't be.'

'It's too late to go all paternal *minister*. I didn't see you riding in on your white horse to play Daddy. You knew it was yours. But you knew it was going to extinguish your rising star. Well, guess what? Your star has burned out.'

He stands up, turns toward her, his face beet red, his hand raised. The driver takes a step towards them. The minister sits back down.

They are quiet, both looking towards the river. A few boats pass upstream leisurely, another world.

'Does he know the child's not his?'

'That's not your business.'

'You've made it all of our business. And what a nasty business it is.'

He stands up, peering down at the river wistfully. Then he lifts his hands up into the air like as if he is about to deliver a barnstorming speech, shakes his head, takes out a cigarette and lights it, takes a long self-satisfied drag.

'Still at that, then?' she says.

'What's it to you?'

'I used to enjoy it too, one of the pleasures we used to share.'

'That's done,' he says, walking towards his driver.

*

The father has always loved the autumn, the painted leaves, the scented chestnuts, and the view from this weather-beaten bench.

He sits alone, watching the tall ships float by on the old meandering river. It hasn't turned cool yet and the wind is perfect for the sailors. The riverside is crowded with tourists from around the world, Europeans, Asians, North and South Americans – all captured by the poetry and fantasy of escape on the high seas.

She was right. He couldn't be counted on to dig a hole deep enough. Though he wonders if she covered the body properly with the mucky soil. But he's thankful for that, for the way it all worked out. The note he tied to the child. The discovery of the body. Prison will suit her, he thinks – the rules, the rigidity. Though she won't like being the one following them rather than setting them. His own brief time in custody after he went to the police was bad enough. It would have been longer, of course, but she insisted she had made all the decisions. No one had a problem believing that.

She was right about the baby, too. It never would have survived, never would have flourished, at least not the way she would have wished. He's not really sure he ever wanted the child, would have preferred aborting it rather than her burying it in the mud – only for it to be dug up by a wet dog on a long leash.

She was right that he didn't know the baby belonged to that fat politician, all puff and polish. Not at first, anyway. She wanted to have it because it was the minister's, naturally. Then she wanted to get rid of it to punish both men, and probably herself. He did know about the affair, the long opening chapter, at least. At first, so many years ago, it stung, her being with that toxic politician, touching him and God knows what else. But he found space for himself in the midst of it. He started to build his own life, slowly over time putting aside a few thousand pounds here, a few thousand pounds there. It began to add up and he bought that two-bed flat near the park, rented it out for years to pay off the mortgage, took up residence there on weekends when he could afford to say no to renters. She was otherwise occupied. He started collecting rare books, bought and sold them, made a few pounds on the side – quite a few pounds, as it turned out.

He's sold them all now, the books, the flat, and the antique shop. Before he sold the books, he pored over an old atlas and plotted a few journeys he'd like to take on his own. Vietnam appealed to him, with its river boats gliding through ancient jungles. He could see himself sitting tall in the back of the boat without a care in the world – without anyone telling him he'd never get it right, never make it to the end of the journey without getting lost.

Anyways, lost is where he wants to be.

He stands up, stretches, takes one final, long gaze across at the river that runs past much of the great city's magic – the Maritime Museum, St. Paul's Cathedral and, of course, Parliament.

A new river will make things right.

As he makes his way out of the park, the father sees a familiar looking man, short, red-haired, standing near the brush where she buried their infant more than a year ago. Is it the policeman? The man is motioning with his hand, crossing himself, crying, shaking, then he falls to his knees.

The father walks quickly towards the weeping man.

Death of a Pacifist

There were thousands of us at Trafalgar Square, chanting in rhythm, 'Don't bomb Syria', then, 'Not in my name'.

A tall, grey-haired black man wearing a navy jacket and cap limped along beside me with the help of a walking stick. He managed to hold a placard in his free hand that shouted: *Who are you are kidding, Mr Cameron?* He had trouble manoeuvring against the late November wind and rain. I tried conversing with him as we marched with the mob of boisterous peace soldiers to Downing Street.

'I'm against the bombing, even if it is that damned Islamic State,' the old man yelled over the whipping wind, his salt and pepper goatee dampening with spittle as he spoke. I caught a hint of Caribbean melodies in his voice. 'Bombing Iraq didn't work. Bombing Afghanistan didn't work. Bombing Libya didn't work. There's no way it's going to sort out Syria.'

'You're right,' I shouted back, though I wasn't sure he could hear me with the protesters around us yelling, blowing referees' whistles and honking horns in the hopes of convincing our fresh-faced Prime Minister to drop his plans to bomb Syria. I didn't really share my marching mate's absolute certainty about Middle East interventions. I just thought bombing Syria was useless, and I was looking to meet up with Serena, the too young bar maid at my local, who said she would see me at Trafalgar Square. She must have been having me on.

'We're just stoking it up. All we'll get out of this is more extremists. Bombing won't make us one bit safer. Probably make things a damn sight worse. Cameron's just a knee jerking jester. And Hilary Benn ...' His voice trailed off as he tried to wipe the rain from his glasses.

Then we got separated in a melee as the Met tried to kettle a roaring crowd of socialists from getting nearer Number 10.

When I got on the train to Blackheath an hour later, the old man plonked himself down across from me, stuck out his long bony right hand and said, 'Fulton – nice to meet you.'

I took his hand. 'Benjamin.'

'Ah, like my bro, Zeph, the poet.'

'I guess,' I laughed.

We talked about poets. He liked the youngsters and their slamming and performance art. I said I admired Wendy Cope and Simon Armitage. He smiled. I told him that I had just bought the bookshop in Blackheath and his eyes lit up like firecrackers.

'Young fellow like you?'

He lived in Blackheath's once-stately Selwyn Court apartments near the station, but leapt up at Lewisham, moving well despite the limp in his left leg.

'See you about, then. Got to go see a girl,' Fulton said, breaking into an expansive smile.

A few days later, he walked into my shop carrying a bundle of books and reached his long arm towards me. 'Fulton, don't suppose you remember.'

The books were bound together in several of those rubber bands that Royal Mail postmen scatter all over our tidy little village in southeast London. Fulton stood so close I could taste the fried onions he'd had for lunch. He beamed, his wiry eyebrows reaching towards his blue cap.

'My book. You're going to sell it.'

I looked it over, trying to show due respect. It was titled *Peace Poet* and it was ninety pages long. The figure on the cover reminded me of a Degas sculpture I had seen at Tate Modern, a man waving a walking stick in silhouette. You couldn't see his face, but the slightly crooked left leg left no doubt it was Fulton. I turned the book over to read the biographical notes.

Fulton left me to it, tapping his way to the new 'Local Authors' shelves I had set up, found a prominent spot for his book of poems, mounted three copies there, and pointed his walking stick at me.

'You've got a bestseller on your hands.'

'We'll see,' I said.

He laughed. 'No doubt, man.'

When he left, I took the books down and put them onto my

backroom desk before rearranging my 'Local Authors'. They were giving me enough grief about selling their tales of woe. I had bought the shop with the help of sizeable loan from my parents, who were spending half the year in the Cayman Islands these days after selling their greeting card business to one of the conglomerates for a small fortune. When I bought it, the little shop had been more like the cramped back office of an eccentric old scholar, complete with cobwebs that had likely been there since the Blitz. I was sprucing it up with new volumes, pine bookshelves and fresh paint. Since my divorce from Loretta, an aspiring model with deep affection for a high life my books couldn't offer, I was living in the tiny flat above the store, basically one rectangular room and a toilet, with wrinkled paperbacks discarded by the former owner scattered throughout.

It took me a week before I turned my attention back to Fulton's book, having moved aside the flyers and spreadsheets that had gathered on my desk. I picked up *Peace Poet* and started reading. An hour later I closed the book and sat for a long time. I had studied poetry at university a decade or so earlier, but I wasn't sure how good Fulton's poems were. They were brave, maybe even foolhardy, mixing politics, religion and sex. However, it was the rhythm that held my attention. I could hear Fulton's hypnotic voice. One phrase struck me:

> *When the river of peace rests in the sea,*
> *It's you, my brother, must take up the plea.*

I locked up the shop and crossed the road for a pint at the Crown. It was all polish and gloss inside, but I preferred the old picnic-style benches outdoors. There was no sign of Serena, and I wasn't sure if she had quit or run off with the waiter with the slicked-back dark hair. I took a long pull of my pint then got out my phone and searched for everything I could find about Fulton. There was more than I had reckoned on: poet, pacifist, church elder, arrested for protesting,

Stephen Lawrence activist, dishwasher and political candidate. The next day I put him back up with the 'Local Authors'.

Fulton was a Windrush baby. Born in Jamaica in the early 1950s, he came to Britain with his parents when he was ten. His daddy drove a bus for fifteen years but got tired of what he called 'harassment' and returned to the Jamaica sunshine. His mum stayed. She'd got a job as a cleaner at Lewisham hospital, worked there for thirty years, washing floors and swabbing down operating theatres, before her body gave out. She collapsed at work, and they shifted her to the A & E, then to a ward, but she only lasted a day. She had a weak heart. Fulton was washing dishes in Brixton at that time, dodging the stop and searches when he left the restaurant in the early morning, six days a week. He told me this when he came by the bookshop a while after we first met, poking his walking stick toward the 'Local Authors', goading me to move his book up to eye level.

'How's it going to be a bestseller when you're hiding it on the bottom shelf?' He was laughing but his stern dark eyes told me was dead serious.

I closed the bookshop for lunch and split my egg salad sandwich with Fulton and made us a pot of tea. He took his black.

'I'm pure,' he said, straight-faced, then added, 'Seriously, it's Martin who made me pure in politics.'

'Martin?'

'Martin Luther King, my one and only hero in this world and the next.'

I wasn't sure what that meant, and so I started rooting around in my rucksack to get my pound cake to split with Fulton, who had devoured his half of the sandwich but hadn't paused to sip his tea.

Suddenly he stood up, took off his cap and held it to his chest and began preaching to his congregation of one, his eyes flashing like a television evangelist.

'I am not unmindful of the fact that violence often brings

about momentary results. Nations have frequently won their independence in battle. But in spite of temporary victories, violence never brings permanent peace.'

He sat down and swallowed his tea in one gulp.

I was too taken aback to speak. I used to have great admiration for Martin Luther King. I wasn't alone. However, I wasn't sure if the American civil rights preacher's precise words would be taken literally in a twenty-first-century Britain that still celebrated its glorious military victories in the great wars of Europe the century before. And, we now had a welfare state, multiculturalism and human rights laws too. Still, I was mindful of the gap between Fulton's life experience and mine, so said nothing.

Fulton, sensing my discomfort, caught my eye and held it, whispering:

'The hottest place in Hell is reserved for those who remain neutral in times of great moral conflict.'

Martin Luther King. I just knew.

As he got up to leave, Fulton said, 'When you have some time, I want to show you something.'

'Okay,' I said, feeling like I owed him.

A week later, we met at the Crown. We drank a pint outside and talked a bit about his poetry. He used odd spellings and liked to twist words like 'machination' into 'machine nations' in his political poems. He also had an affection for alliteration. He talked too about how distressed he was during the Brixton riots in the eighties, how he almost went and got himself a brick or a can of petrol to join in the struggle.

'But it just wasn't me. Mum was starting to get sick, though she never told anyone. I knew. I had to stay close to her and I wouldn't have been able to live with myself if I had left her to go into battle with a brick.'

'Have you faced racism?' I heard my voice breaking.

'Benjamin,' he scolded. 'This is a racist country. See that crooked leg. They kicked me every day at school for years, from the moment I arrived on that boat. I tried to fit in. We all tried. But once *they* got us here, got us to drive their buses, scrub their floors and wash their dishes, *they* never wanted anything to do with us. I love this place. I've never left. I'm not going back to Jamaica, though my daddy's there – eighty-three years old! But this country can be Hell for a man with my skin. You can let it infect you. Some people do. I choose love and poetry over sticks and stones.'

I was trying to figure out if Fulton thought I was part of the *they*. I wondered, too, how Fulton would see my mum and dad, soaking up the Cayman sun behind locked gates in a pristine neighbourhood in his part of the world.

He stood up.

'One more pint, then I'm taking you somewhere.'

I didn't resist.

Five minutes' walk from the Crown to the heath and another five minutes' hike and we arrived at a scruffy bit of elevated brush and bushes. Fulton stopped, lifted his stick towards the sky, closed his eyes and shushed me. 'Listen.'

There was a swirl of wind, a jet headed to Heathrow, a helicopter twirling towards the Thames, then nothing. Not a bird. Not a dog. No kids. Like he had willed it. Then Fulton whispered, 'Can you hear them?'

'Uh, no. Fulton, are you taking the piss here ...'

'Hush.'

I didn't hear anything. But at least I knew not to laugh.

Suddenly, Fulton started preaching towards the heavens. It was like Martin Luther King's sermon, back in my little office, but eerie, his voice wobbling like he had lost control of it.

'When Adam delved and Eve span, who was then the gentleman? From the beginning all men by nature were created alike, and our bondage or servitude came in by the unjust oppression of naughty men. For if God would have had any bondmen from the beginning, he would have appointed who should be bond, and who free. And, therefore I exhort you to consider that now the time is come, appointed to us by God, in which ye may (if ye will) cast off the yoke of bondage, and recover liberty.'

He stopped. There were tears in his eyes. He was in a kind of trance. We stood there for a long time before he spoke.

'Do you know who that was?'

'Not Martin Luther King.'

'Not Martin.'

'Who was it?'

I was wary of where we were heading, worried about Fulton's expression, the tears, the sweat rolling down his face, his shaking.

'I hear those words when I come here,' Fulton said, reading my mind. 'That's John Ball. They've got a school in Blackheath named after him, though I'm bloody certain they don't know what he was about. He was preaching to the rebels in the Peasants' Revolt on this very spot in 1381.

'This was Wat Tyler's Mound. You know him? It's also known as Whitefield's Mound, one of the first Methodists. My mum and daddy's families were all Methodists. In 1739, Whitefield preached to 20,000 people – here!

'They were for justice, these people. The Chartists came here too. You know who they were? And then came the suffragists – nonviolent women changing the world for the better. Some men yelled at them, "You're just telling the same old story." Smart women, they agreed: "And we're going to keep on telling the story."

'Benjamin,' Fulton said, looking down at his crooked leg. 'This old body is getting weary. Guys like you have got to take up the story, like those youngsters following me around – bring justice, jobs, equality to this country – and without violence.'

Quiet.

'That's why I brought you to the mound – it's holy ground.'

In the weeks that followed I thought a lot about what happened at the mound, all the things Fulton had been trying to teach me. Still, I wondered how many of us had time to wage his kind of peaceful war, with the need to work and the time-consuming act of just living. I wasn't sure how he paid his bills though I know his mum had left him something – and he sold his books in stores across South East London. I was drawn to Fulton as a man of character and as a storyteller, but I wondered if he really knew me and my lack of principles. I was too busy trying to get my bookshop to turn a profit while Mum and Dad in the Cayman Islands were pressuring me to shut it.

Good Friday was coming at the elegant church on the heath I attended sporadically – too many 'bells and smells' and not enough meat in the preaching. It was Mum and Dad's church, really, though I wondered why. The vicar, who was nearing retirement, had announced he was going to hold a service on something called 'just wars.' The bishop wanted congregations to think about the gas attacks in Syria and the recent calls for British air strikes. Good thing Mum and Dad weren't here for this, but I was at least curious.

The Sunday before, I had mentioned the service to Fulton when I saw him heading to the mound with a group of youngsters he was helping find work. One of them, a plump young fellow with a retro afro, had been sleeping on Fulton's sofa after the old poet had got him to turn his knife in, change his ways. The youngsters were making a racket, so I wasn't sure Fulton heard me.

There were no more than twenty of us seated down the left side of the church, the rest of it shrouded in tarpaulins thanks to the never-ending renovations to the imposing old edifice. I sat close to the front of the church. The frail vicar was known to mumble. After a few short prayers, the vicar put up a list of the 'Seven Principles of a Just War' on a flipchart. He started talking about number one, 'Last Resort'.

Suddenly Fulton tapped his way to the front of the church. I hadn't known he was there, but when I saw him I thought he was trying to get a closer look at the words printed on the flipchart. Fulton then turned around to face the congregation and started chanting. The vicar sat down.

I didn't take in everything he had to say in the few minutes he had our attention before two elders escorted him from the church. I was too worried about the way he looked, cap askew, jacket covered in leaves, shoes muddy. Had he been sleeping rough? He ran through the vicar's litany in one mocking breath – last resort, legitimate authority, just cause, probability of success, right intention, proportionality, civilian casualties – shook his head and sang:

'It's love, not hate. Appreciate.

Some wars okay? What more, I say?

Adultery? Good God, you say.

Bible tells us to love and pray.

Jesus said love your enemy.'

As the elders near carried him out of the stunned gathering, Fulton hollered, 'I've been thrown out of better places in Alabama with Martin Luther King. We carry on the struggle.'

The vicar got up to continue his talk, but I left my pew in search of Fulton. I wanted to see if he was alright. He was setting out across the heath with a few of his youngsters when I caught up to him.

'Fulton, you don't look so good.'

'Book man, Benjamin. The truth is things are happening. I've got to sort it. I might need your help. I'll let you know. Your vicar, man . . .' He just shook his head.

There was something bugging me.

'You told me you've never left Britain since you arrived from Jamaica?'

He gave me a long stare, like he was trying to remember what he had told me. 'Marching with Martin. You're talking about Alabama,' he responded finally.

'Well?'

'I was with him in my dreaming and scheming – and he's marching with me today. That's my "just marching" theory,' he laughed, turning to walk away, his oak stick pointing towards the mound.

I didn't know what to think of Fulton's explanation. I walked home pondering his cheek, half worried he was headed off into some kind of personal and political madness.

I only saw Fulton once or twice over the next year. I was

fighting to save my business. Mum and Dad had sent their consultant – the one who had sold their greeting-card business – to sort things out. I agreed to talk to him. It was either that or I would lose the line of credit they had set up for my bookshop. Things were getting tense and I didn't want to lose the store after working at it for a year.

I guessed Fulton was busy too. He came by the bookshop collecting for the Grenfell fire families. He and his band were making up packets of clothes, books and toiletries with 1960s peace signs stamped on them. I gave him a few quid and a couple of paperbacks. His books were selling, and I was sending the money on. I asked him about the problem he mentioned after the Good Friday service, that he might need my help, and he said he'd be in touch. He moved more slowly than I remembered; he was quieter, possibly distracted.

'Keep the faith,' Fulton called back over his shoulder.

A month later, I happened to meet Fulton having a pint outside the Crown with his woman friend, Maxine. I had seen them around the village on occasion and he introduced me to her as they sipped a pint.

I'd given up looking for Serena and she no longer answered my texts, though I still saw her boyfriend, the waiter, who smiled at me knowingly when I ran into him at the pub. I had seen Fulton and Maxine together a few times over the months, crossing the heath, his arms gesticulating wildly, her laughing alongside him. She was probably in her forties, not that much older than me, smartly dressed at the pub wearing a rainbow scarf and long, dangling earrings. I sipped my pint, listening to Fulton talk about helping some peace church send people to Israel and Palestine to stand between the two sides to prevent another Intifada. I couldn't keep my eyes off Maxine. I was watching her watching him. Her dark eyes seemed to change colour slightly moment by moment, probably reflecting the sun peeking in and out of the clouds, but somehow illustrating her complicated attachment to the old poet – changing from awe to amusement to worry. I was seeing the different faces of the poet – through her eyes.

Then I looked directly at Fulton. He always seemed to be able to suss out different approaches to political problems. So, I was happy to hear that some churches weren't just sending pilgrims on Holy Land tours or praying for the end times. Those days seemed close enough. Fulton was obsessed with never using a gun or a bomb to help settle things. I never really had the gall or the energy to argue with him about whether that was the only approach, though he knew I was somewhat cynical of his so-called path of peace.

Then Maxine asked, 'Fulton, love, what happened to your peacemakers when Hitler was murdering and massacring across Europe? It was men with big guns and bigger bombs that ended that. Your Martin Luther King ways might not always work, you know.'

Fulton put his pint down quietly, stared at me as I picked a few last grains of salt from the bottom of my peanuts packet. It was almost like he was accusing me of putting Maxine up to it, suggesting I didn't have the nerve to ask that question. He was right, of course. Fulton grabbed his walking stick from where it was leaning against the picnic bench as if he was going to leave, but just gripped it and responded in a slow, clear tone.

'Give peacemakers the human resources, the big budgets, the broad political will, business's push, organized labour's blessing, the spiritual guidance of the holy church, the great nationalistic fervour of every living man, woman and child to the very end – like you had in that bloody war – and then we'll see how things compare.'

He stood up and went off to the loo.

Maxine turned her dark eyes toward me and shook her head, and again said what I was thinking: 'He's thought it through, but I don't know ...'

A few days later I got this text from Fulton: *Meet me at the mound.*

I wish now that I had understood how desperate he was.

I was trying to keep the bookshop alive, so shutting early wasn't possible, and a few last-minute customers were rummaging through the sales bins for weather-worn Richard Ford or Katherine Mansfield paperbacks. I couldn't just kick them out.

I will always regret not getting there sooner.

When I arrived at the mound, Fulton's body lay among the thick greenery, arms and legs spread out like a mangled human clock, a ring of yellow high-vis police officers surrounding him. His blue navy cap rested on the ground beside him, his oak walking stick lying further off.

Beyond the circle stood a ragtag cluster of a dozen youngsters with heads hung low, carrying home-made placards declaring, *Free Fulton*.

It was as if I had walked on to a Ken Loach film set, though the wailing of the ambulance and police cars as they mounted the kerb and drove across the heath told me otherwise.

Fulton was dead, and, though it took me some time to admit it to myself, maybe a part of me had died too. I would hesitate to say exactly what part that was, confusing as that sounds.

A few weeks after the inquest I closed the bookshop for lunch – there wasn't much lunchtime trade and it increasingly looked like I might have to shut the place down permanently. Mum and Dad were coming home for a spell and wanted a meeting with me and their consultant. It didn't look good and I didn't know what I would do with myself if I lost the bookshop. I strolled the few hundred yards across the heath to the mound. It was a sunny afternoon, but there were dark clouds in the distance. I stood on the edge of the few square meters of odd tufts of grasses and weedy bushes that had become a blight to most heath walkers but for me had become a kind of monument to that mad poet.

When Fulton first brought me here to listen for the voices of the revolutionary John Ball, the holy Wesleyans, the peaceful suffragists, I could only hear the wind. I stood a long time, but again heard nothing but that wind and one annoying crow telling me to buzz off back to my bookshop. But I couldn't get Fulton out of my mind – his poetry, his politics, his twisted body lying on the mound. Tears started rolling down my cheeks and I began to shiver violently. The episode lasted less than a minute. But it shook me to the core.

The inquest lasted only a day. It was his heart that killed him. That's what they said. Fulton had a condition that meant any excitement might have set it off. His doctor admitted this under some intense questioning from the Met's lawyers. The coroner said the Taser was probably misused and admonished the officer wielding it. Still, the coroner emphasized that Fulton had escalated the situation by 'waving his walking stick about and theatrically reaching towards his jacket pocket', though he acknowledged Fulton carried no weapon and had been trying to show the police the latest document he had received from the Home Office, telling him he was in the country illegally – after living here for fifty years. And the coroner maintained that the fact that some of Fulton's ragtag followers had put out messages on social media that Fulton would be defending his right to remain in Britain 'to the very end' had created a kind of 'inhospitable environment' and that the police were right to be there in numbers – and to have the Taser at hand.

When I read all this in the newspaper, in black and white, it was hard to argue with. Bad heart? Inhospitable environment? It made sense. Still, I thought, the police didn't know Fulton, the coroner didn't know Fulton and the reporter covering the inquest didn't know Fulton. I did. I have to admit that he was bloody annoying at times, preaching like Martin Luther King, disrupting our Good Friday church service, pushing me to sell his thin volume of poetry, dropping hints about his troubles but never letting me know how I could help.

Occasionally, he even stretched the truth a bit to make a point. But he wouldn't have swatted away a mosquito – even with his gnarly old walking stick – let alone attack a police officer. Weak heart? Maybe. But Fulton, though he limped through his life in this part of the city, rarely strayed from the path he thought was right. I wasn't sure anyone could have said the same about all those officials at the inquest. Or whether I could have said the same about myself. I was too busy trying make a living to see the crooked old man dying right in front of me. That's what really hurt, to be honest.

Halfway back to my bookshop, I stopped in my tracks as I heard those wailing police sirens again at the mound. I looked over my shoulder and, sure enough, a police van was arriving at the kerb near the mound, and six or seven officers climbed out of it, strapping on helmets and grabbing shields – like ancient warriors preparing to do battle. A ragged group of Fulton's peace army was marching in from Greenwich Park in groups of threes and fours, waving their placards. I think they were yelling, 'Stay out of Iran' and I could hear his name being shouted too: 'Fulton lives. Fulton lives.'

Though, of course, he was dead. I'd seen him with my own eyes.

Fulton always said there were those who benefited from continuous war and that we ought to be persistent in seeking peaceful ways out of our messes. I had my doubts, though I probably should have argued that point with him. The youngsters, however, must have thought another war was coming and they were resisting in their own noisy and undisciplined way. I looked at them on the heath and didn't know what to think.

'Peace is the only answer, and it starts right here,' Fulton had told me many times over the past year or so, pounding his chest.

'That's just sloganeering,' I always replied.

'No,' he'd say. 'That's the truth. Peace starts in your own heart – but it needs to burst out into the real world, otherwise it shrinks you, suffocates you.'

Maybe I should have joined Fulton's band on the mound; maybe those kids shouldn't have been left on their own to make change. I was worried they would end up like Fulton, lifeless among the weeds.

Maybe.

But there was going to be trouble and I had enough of that

on my plate. It was going to be a battle to keep my bookshop running and I needed all my business artillery to win that fight. One of the big chains had opened a bookshop in the village and shoppers evidently liked the look of the place – branded like a local bookshop with an old-fashioned sign out front, funnily enough – and the price of the books. I figured that was the only fight I truly had energy for, but I wasn't optimistic about winning. The odds were against me.

I turned away from Fulton's followers and walked towards my bookshop. A man carrying a black leather case stood outside the display window where I had recently placed Fulton's *Peace Poet*. My mum and dad, looking richly tanned and in their best business outfits, but grim and determined, greeted him with cordial handshakes and chat as they peered inside the store where Fulton's shadowy figure dominated my latest window display.

'So it begins,' I thought as I walked towards them, feeling ripped in two, one part of me preparing my best arguments for keeping the bookshop alive, the other part haunted by Fulton's verse:

> *When the river of peace rests in the sea,*
> *It's you, my brother, must take up the plea.*

Too Old for *Scandal*

For Rod

Duke sipped his pint, eyeing Rusty, the bar man, who was wiping down the scuffed tables at the Somerset pub.

The elderly patron waited patiently for the bar man's inevitable question.

On Tuesday nights the retired teacher was usually surrounded by his mates. Duke knew for sure Rusty would be curious where they all had got to.

Soon the question came.

'Where are they all? What's the gossip?' Rusty asked.

Duke understood the bar man was well placed behind the Somerset bar pulling pints most days to know a great deal of what was happening around the pub. However, he enjoyed the fact that the red-haired bar man didn't know everything that was going on. Duke smiled as he sipped his pint.

'No gossip, just one of those nights. We're too old for scandal,' he quipped.

Duke finished his lager, left the bar, turned right past the old nick, newly polished-up as flats for old folks, and headed towards Sainsbury's on the edge of the village to buy chicken for his dinner, stewing over a recent conversation he'd recently had. He'd been doing that a lot recently. But this conversation held him somehow.

*

In the scruffy garden of the Somerset, Duke nursed a pint, dragging on another cigarette. Out of the smoky haze, sweet-scented Terri suddenly plonked herself down on the bench beside him. She wore her grey hair down for a change, her open denim jacket offering up the deep brown shades of her Greek-island tan.

Whistle, Terri's salt-and-pepper Schnauzer, snuggled up to her skinny jeans.

'I thought I might join you for a half,' Terri said, setting down her glass and wrapping Whistle's leash around the bench. 'How're you doing, Duke?' she asked in that husky voice Rusty sometimes mimicked, giving the geezers at the bar a laugh.

Terri had known Duke for years. They were both active in

local party politics, bumped into each other at the village market on Sundays and met at the Somerset, the once-majestic pub a few minutes' walk from the heart of the village. She hadn't seen much of him since his wife, Mags, got struck down by the demon cancer that first hit a few years ago and kept lashing out at new parts of her debilitated body, finally claiming an unholy victory nine months ago.

Duke reached across to gently pet Whistle. 'It is what it is,' he said, taking a long drag on his cigarette before taking another sip of his lager.

Terri touched his arm.

'You do know,' she persisted, 'if you ever need company, a hot meal or a cup o' tea ... or an indecent hug ...'

Duke frowned.

'Don't give me that look, Duke. We've been friends too long. And leave Mick out of it.'

Mick was Terri's husband, wheelchair-bound for years and now in a home a thirty-minute bus ride away, already left out of so many of the good things in life by a kind of cruel arthritic fate.

Duke scowled, got up and went to the gents. He finished his business, washed his hands, grimacing at the grey mirror image, then wandered slowly back outside to his half-finished pint.

Terri was gone. He'd probably get a text later apologizing. It wasn't the first time he had sensed Terri had wanted to rescue him from the pit of his mourning. This time she had aimed her little arrows straight for the tiny crack she saw in his armour – a decent meal, a steaming cup of tea, and the hint of a sexual encounter. It wasn't that he wasn't tempted but ... no.

*

Making his way home for his chicken dinner, Duke was thinking back to when the three of them – Terri, Mags and himself – ran into each other at a fundraiser for Labour years ago. Terri's flair caught Duke's eye back then, but Mags' studious nature eventually won him over. The three of them would get together for drinks or go for an Indian near the heath. When Terri got together with Mick a year later, they became pretty close, 'a fearsome back four', Duke used to call them. How they'd laugh at that.

Terri had run for Council a few years ago. She got beaten badly. She was smart enough to manage the hospital's social work team before retiring, but people seemed to dismiss her for not looking the part. For being female and pretty.

Terri was good to talk to, unless it was politics. She was too far 'out there' for Duke, wanting to nationalize every damn thing. Books made better banter for them. She read widely and remembered what she'd read. Duke was losing that ability, though he still devoured Ian Rankin novels, Val McDermid too. He shied away from the so-called 'literary' stuff after teaching teenagers *Great Expectations* for decades. He'd had enough of it somehow.

There had been a few flickers of romance between Duke and Terri over the years, moments he might have succumbed to the fragrance of her gardenia perfume, the bright colours she wore to enticing effect. She was friendly, prone to expressing herself by placing her manicured fingers on Duke's arm. He was often tempted to test the limits of their flirtation – but nothing happened. They were both in what everyone would say were good marriages, though both couples had separated for a stretch at different times. Terri once left Mick because of his hard drinking but went back to him when his rheumatoid arthritis started to degenerate, and never left him again. Fifteen years ago, Duke spent a bank-holiday weekend with a student teacher; Mags knew what was up and locked him out when he came home. It took a long time but, somehow, they patched things up. Things were good after that. For both couples.

Duke was reminiscing about all this as he baked the chicken in the oven, cooked the rice, chopped some carrots and broccoli, dropping them into boiling water in the saucepans Mags got at John Lewis. Mags would have followed one of Nigella's recipes. She would have also offered him advice on any dilemma he was trying to deal with. He missed that.

Washing up after dinner, Duke hummed quietly. He and Mags used to do the washing up together, singing Beatles tunes, sometimes Gerry and the Pacemakers. He missed that too. Still, despite all those memories, Duke was slowly growing to appreciate his tidy new flat near the station. There was no point in keeping that big house. He was slowly living into his new independence, yet still talking to Mags. Though he never let on. The kids were in America and they'd each call every fortnight but kept things cheerful, perhaps fearing Duke would get weepy. His brother on the coast would check how Charlton Athletic Football Club – the Addicks – were doing, made Duke feel things might get back to some kind of normal. It wouldn't bring back Mags, though. He knew that. Of course, he did.

Duke collapsed into the comfortable leather chair Mags bought him for his retirement, closed his eyes and let his thoughts drift back to that conversation with Terri. She had always been direct, tactile, when they talked politics or books. But this was different: her tone, her hand on his arm, her tanned breasts ...

*

The next Tuesday, the crew were at the Somerset. Duke was first. Solly arrived a few minutes later, brought his lager outside, taking off his fedora and rubbing his hands through the few remaining white hairs on his oversized head.

'If they let that blond bastard into Number 10, I'll move to France. It'll be the end of us. He can't keep it in his boxers long enough to Brexit! How's he going to run the bloody country ...'

Solly's voice faded out as the wind picked up in the back garden and traffic on the busy street ground to a halt. The rest of the Tuesday-evening crowd wandered over to the bench at the back of the garden. Duke, Solly and Doreen were smokers, so everyone gathered outside as the three of them inhaled the blue smoke. Solly, who used to run the village art gallery, had an affair years ago with Doreen, a translator who worked for the government.

'She wanted me to travel the world with her,' Solly once confessed to Duke. 'Angela got wind of it and straightened me out – right quick. Still ...'

Terri arrived with her neighbour, Sandro, a chef from Italy working in the pizza place in the village. It was his night off. Sandro had a young wife and a new baby. Terri had invited him along, thinking Sandro's wife didn't let him out enough.

Sandro was saying, 'Even if they say I have a "special skill" and let me stay, I think I will go back to Italy. I would rather be unemployed in Genoa than treated like shit in this pseudo-empire.'

'The point is,' Doreen interjected sternly, 'We'll all be better off if we stay within the natural boundaries of our cultural, religious, and political contexts. We've wandered away ...'

Solly roared, 'You're just telling Sandro to fuck off back to Italy in your ever-so-piss-elegant way ...'

Duke got up, pointing like a mime to his empty pint glass, and headed inside to get another beer, and to see if he could chat with Rusty about football, anything but Brexit.

Rusty was laying out the free grub to keep the punters drinking. Duke settled onto a bar stool, turned to look out at the traffic when Terri suddenly appeared.

'I'm headed *home*,' she said, her blue eyes freezing him.

'Without Sandro?' Duke responded.

'He'll find his way back.'

'Okay.'

'Will *you*?'

Duke didn't answer because Sandro had just joined them at the bar. They chatted about the new Mike Leigh film. Terri was getting a group together to go on seniors' afternoon.

Duke said he had to leave and left them waiting for Rusty to lay out the egg sandwiches and salt and vinegar crisps. Duke avoided looking at Terri. She was wearing that denim jacket, buttoned up to her neck, very prim.

*

Twenty years ago, Mick would sometimes tag along with Duke when he travelled to the Valley to see Charlton Athletic play. Mick preferred rugby, but Duke would sometimes get an extra ticket. Good-hearted – unless you were talking politics – Mick would always surrender. The matches were dire, at one point with Charlton going thirteen matches without a win.

Mick had begun suffering from the crippling arthritis and used to complain that he was freezing to death in the second half on those harsh winter Saturday afternoons. Duke would pull a red scarf from his Charlton rucksack, saying, 'This will keep you warm.'

A few days after abandoning Terri and Sandro at the Somerset, Duke took the bus to visit Mick at the care home. Duke hadn't been since Mags had started her last journey that ended in her death last year. When Duke walked into the sparse third-floor room overlooking the carpark, Mick looked up languidly from his crossword. He was as pale as his bed sheets, looked more like a refugee from some foreign war zone than the Mick he knew so well. Gone was the fire-in-the-belly journalist who would bang out columns on the idiocy of Westminster.

'Brought you something,' Duke said after a long pause, pulling the fluffy red scarf from his jacket pocket. 'Winter's coming.'

He was hoping for a laugh.

Mick started sobbing.

Duke stood there, silent, immobile.

Finally, Mick stopped crying and managed to get the scarf around his neck and feebly warbled, 'Come on, you reds!'

For a while they sipped mugs of tea and Duke replayed the Brexit banter from the Somerset and Mick laughed sadly. Soon Duke saw he was weary, reached for his jacket.

'You didn't come to talk about Brexit,' Mick said.

'Why do you say that?'

'How long have we known each other?'

'Quite a few seasons.'

'I've been injured for the last couple ...'

'I should have been here more ...'

'That's not it, mate. You had Mags to look after.'

'What, then?'

'It's the final whistle for me.'

'Come on, Mick ...'

'I want you to look after Terri,' Mick whispered sharply.

'What do you mean?'

Duke could feel his face redden, just like Rusty at the Somerset.

Mick just waved Duke away.

Duke turned and left the room.

He'd talk it through with Mags at home.

*

Another Tuesday came. Duke, Solly and Doreen smoked outside in the damp evening air, then moved in to join Terri and Sandro. Terri handed out the film tickets and they had another round.

Duke left early. An hour later he had settled onto his easy chair with fish and chips from the nearby 'bespoke' chippy. He turned on his television. Charlton were two goals down.

When the doorbell rang, he got up quickly, spilling several vinegar-drenched chips onto the carpet. He could hear Mags tutting as he opened the door to a wind-blown Terri.

'You look like Dorothy, blown off course on her way back to Kansas,' he managed to mutter.

'Let me in, Duke. I'm freezing.'

He was slow to respond so she walked around him, went to the loo to dry herself off, came out a few moments later, pink-faced from Duke's rough bathroom towel. Duke stood there looking at her.

Terri was uncharacteristically silent as she methodically shed her raincoat, denim jacket, blouse, bra... in the middle of Duke's living room.

*

Mick died a few months later and the crew joined Terri at the Somerset after the funeral. It was bitter outdoors, so they gathered in a corner under the television showing horse-racing. They sat quietly, sipping their drinks. Every so often Solly or Doreen would start up: 'Remember that column Mick wrote about Margaret Thatcher ...'

Duke braved the bitter outdoors for a cigarette, pulling on his weathered woolly Charlton hat to keep himself warm as he sat on the damp bench thinking about Mick, then letting his thoughts wander to the night Terri visited, about how he had rarely made love for so long or laughed so hard; how his gnarly old hands explored the rich Greek-island tan that covered Terri's petite body; how he couldn't wash off the scent of her for days; how he knew that night was both the beginning and the end of the affair; how he didn't regret it, not one bit.

He stubbed his cigarette, drained his pint and wandered back into the Somerset.

The Tuesday crew were gone. Rusty offered Duke another pint on the house. But there was a cost. Rusty leaned across the damp bar mats, whispering, 'What's happening with your lot, Duke?' Duke shook his head like he had no idea.

The truth was, he did know. Terri had put her house on the market and was moving to Italy with Sandro. A few days before Mick's funeral, she had sent Duke a note, apologizing for 'that lovely, lusty, loony night' and told him about her plans. Duke hadn't been surprised. Sandro had put a smile on Terri's face. And that was good to see.

On top of that, Somerset regulars were whispering that on some late nights, Solly and Doreen were getting together at the wine bar in the village. Rusty had probably heard that too, wanted confirmation. Duke didn't know for sure if that was happening. In any case, he thought, 'It is what it is.'

Duke turned to Rusty and said, 'Nothing new, mate. We're all too old for scandal.'

Rusty shook his red head and wiped down the pockmarked bar.

Duke left the Somerset huddled inside his winter coat with a grim smile across his shivering grey face. He was restless to get home for a cup of tea, anxious too to have one last conversation with Mags about it all.

Areas Requiring Attention

Winter

I hold it like my baby, press it close to my breast, hug it, kiss it, talk to it, smell it, listen to it, feel it, love it ... You never understood such commitment, never tried to, took off before I could explain it to you, lay it all out for you, cause like that Country and Western song says, you're just a *man* ... That girl you went to, the one perched on those sexy red high heels, the one with the puffed-up lips you couldn't keep yours off, the one you said made you dizzy with ... God knows what – literary delight? ... Daddy did that too, took off at the first whiff of French perfume, or was it American kitsch with a foreign name, scripted in some Arabic-looking italics? Had to *find* himself ... So *deep*, such a time of *discovery*, but now he knows the secret of happiness is not found in the crack of a woman's arse ... A lot of good that does him at that piss-stained care home up north... You're just like him ... Mum used to tell me that ... 'Stop fixing on that boy with the sexy slouch, the sweet talk, the hand on the back of your neck, the other one groping through your purse' ... Too late for such sage advice ... I had already *accidentally* tripped over you in the English Lit stacks that bitter January day, taken you to Starbucks (of all the tacky places, everything colour-coordinated, matching perfectly, except the prices and my income, not that you cared a jot), stripped off in the elevator of your dingy building because it got you in the mood before we opened the door of your unkempt flat with books scattered everywhere, like you'd actually read them, held you in the shower when you cried because your novel was rejected – again – poor baby, how you raged like a spoiled brat when I introduced you to something called 'third-person narration', sorry, forgot your favourite word is 'I' ... I won't let go of it, want to feel it throbbing in my hands, hear it sing a new song to me, tell me a story with a fresh script, tell me the truth, or a lie, I don't care, but tell me that I don't just need, want, fear, loathe, that I am ... I don't know, wanted, loved, or just bloody *am* ... Doctor doesn't have a couch, teaches breathing and meditation with candles and violin music I recognize from somewhere (Daddy's care home?), telling me it's time to forgive, even bloody forget, start over, if only I had a pill for every time I've heard that, such bullshit I get from new-age gurus and AA addicts ... Then the doctor puts his hand on my knee, what a surprise, 'See you next week', everything's normal, perfectly framed family photo on his paper-free desk, like fuck, more, 'See you in court, good doctor', just give me the pills you promised, the ones that blur my reality, though they don't matter, I already have my love, my life, my hope, resting in my hand ... Just ring ...

Spring

I want you to know I'm better now. There's no need to call. Your card was lovely, very touching. Much appreciated. You're right, the new doctor is wonderful. She has a lot of experience dealing with my particular 'issue', as you so aptly put it. We haven't discussed the other doctor yet, but we will soon. We promised each other we would. I think she wants me off all medication and we are working towards that goal, one day at a time. She says that a lot. I am starting to say it too. I think I get it. I was happy to hear about your new book. It sounds interesting. Of course, I don't mind you writing about our relationship, fictionalized, of course, reshaped, I think you said. Thanks for asking. It doesn't surprise me that the early reviews have called it 'brave'. You always were brave with your writing. I know you dedicated it to her. It makes sense. It doesn't bother me at all. I told Mum about your book and she seemed pleased. She didn't say a great deal but seemed happy that you finished your book. I told her I was working on one too and she congratulated me. It made me feel good. I have written twenty thousand words and I think it reads well. It would be great if you could look it over, but perhaps that's not such a good idea. No, I won't send it. You will be happy to know that I visit Mum now. It had been a long time. I don't mind her little cottage anymore and she has a new man, a butcher who spends his days off tinkering with antique tractors. She seems to like him. They laugh a lot, talk politics, but don't goad me about my alternative views. I just listen, watch them being happy. It's amazing, really. Mum encourages me to go see Daddy, so I do, every fortnight or so. Yesterday, he sat up for half an hour and sipped a cup of tea with me and even took a bite of digestive biscuit. I hadn't seen him so cheerful in a long time. I think they cleaned the care home up a bit. It might have been after that inspection. I'm pleased you agreed I should file the complaint. The staff are friendlier. That could be down to the new manager. You can probably tell I've stopped drinking. It's for the best. The new doctor tells me this. I have to agree with her. I'm no longer on that dating site either. I don't miss it at all. There were too many questionable types, 'creeps', you called them. You may be right, especially that one guy. It's not worth saying any more about him. The doctor says we might talk about it in a few weeks or so but that it's up to me. But I'm feeling strong now, working again, writing a little most days, seeing family. Spring is in the air. I'm not sure it would be good to revisit that 'date'. It's water under the bridge. Is that the right expression? I don't know.

Summer

I called you. The other day. Okay, six times. Maybe more. I'm not sure. Not sure about anything. Why haven't you answered? Why can't you talk to me for five minutes? Just sort things out. Okay, I heard you're getting married. It's not that. Okay, maybe partly. How could you marry that pseudo-intellectual with Botox lips? Did she ever finish that book of short stories? Really, nobody is writing those Karl Ove Knausgaard factual fantasy memoirs any more ... God, she made the madwoman a blonde with a lisp instead of a brunette with an overbite like mine. Genius. Captures the universality of insanity, I'm sure ... Eat your heart out, Karl Ove! What's she calling it, *A String of Lies*? Fits. I hope she's not pregnant. Never mind. It's not about *her*. It's not about her marrying *you*. Definitely not. It's more. Your book. Yes, I have been rereading it. Close reading, I can hear you correcting, editing me still. Guess what? I have been editing you. That's why I want to meet up with you. Show you. The edited version of your book. Ha, ha, ha. It reminds me of Daddy's old Bible. He went through and underlined all the parts about poverty, justice, that sort of thing. Amazing, ruined his Bible. But gave him mountains of good sermons. Yeah, I know, he was also sleeping with the red-haired soprano in the senior choir. The one with the French perfume. That's a different story. He's still paying for that. Rightly so. Your book, what's it called? Oh, yes, *The Feast*. Your feast. My hunger. You, feasting on my love for you. Okay, I hear you, even from here. My *obsession* with you. All great works of literature are rooted in ... Blah, blah, blah. My copy is littered with yellow edits. What did you used to call them? 'Areas Requiring Attention'. I don't want to go into detail. Not now. Just one thing, though. I never said your writing inspired me to make love with you. It isn't that good. And neither is your sex. There, I said it. You know there is a difference between slow and comatose, right? I can hear your *writer* voice, 'Don't forget this is fiction, it has its own set of rules and permeations.' Blah, blah, blah. Another thing. I didn't really want to do this now. But here goes. I did not 'sleep around' before I met you. How did you put it? 'It would be irresponsible of me to suggest that she came to my bed without having previously mastered her numerous earlier tutorials on elegant French numerology.' Does anybody actually talk like that? And you know bloody well there was just that one guy in high school. We got drunk on cheap wine at his parents' seaside flat that summer, very posh. You and that pop tart would love it. And the teacher. I told you! Fuck. He. Raped. Me. After that British Museum class outing to see the 'Women and Colonialism' exhibit. Said he would help me home after I twisted my ankle. Said he needed to phone the taxi from his friend's place. Told me a hot bath would do me good. Told me he would get me a towel. Told me so many lies. How could you twist that? Fictionalise my reality? Violate me again? You bastard. Never mind a conversation. It's too late. You said you'd always love me. You lied. Your book is full of lies. I never want to talk to you. I hate you. You are dead. To me.

Autumn

I think you'd like this place. It's a *The Remains of the Day* kind of home surrounded by acres of blessed greenery, so pastoral, reminds me of the cover of that Thomas Hardy book you loaned me when we started dating. We have vegetable patches, maple trees, a falling-down barn, but no sheep. I've always loved Hardy, but you found him too ... what was the word? 'Unpolished', I think. Maybe because he never studied Creative Writing like you did. Poor fellow. It's just a joke, don't mind me. This place is in the city, but I can't hear any traffic and even the jets seem distant as they arc towards Gatwick. Thank God, Mum sold the cottage and was able to pay for this, my month in the country. Sounds like a short story title, 'My Month in the Country'. Don't steal it. You were always taking my ideas, arguing that you had the skills to turn them into great literature. That's probably true. Mum sold the cottage so she could fly off to Paris with that famous chef she met in Cornwall. A step up, you'd say. But I liked the butcher, an honest, straightforward fellow, not vague and puffy like some men I know. It's just a joke, don't mind me. Here at my village funny farm in the middle of the bad old city, we eat three healthy meals a day. My bowels function like clockwork. I sleep eight hours straight every night. There's no alcohol, the medications are strictly administered. As they should be. We've checked our mobile phones, laptops and sundry technological devices at the front desk. They are under lock and key until we leave. Or are released? Just joking. You know me. That's why you will read this last note with all my frilly handwriting. You used to love my 'script' when I sent you those poems about my broken, bleeding, bloated heart. That seems such a long time ago. Another country, one I'm still exploring. I prefer the group to the one-on-one sessions. You can never really hide here but in group you can get by with a lot of nodding and 'Thanks for sharing that' kind of talk. One-on-one is scary. No hands on the knee here but questions like darts hitting the bullseye. Piercing. Of course, I knew that Daddy was sleeping around. Yes, I begged him not to go, ripped the suitcase out of his hand that bleak fall morning, wind and rain rattling the windows as the taxi took him away, while upstairs Mum slept in their queen-sized bed. No, I don't want to tell you how the fuck it made me feel. Figure it out. Sorry. Not you. That's what I tell the doctor, I mean, 'Jason', as he insists. I am feeling better. At least I think I am. Some days I feel nothing. That's the drugs, Jason explains. It seems to make sense when he says it. We'll wean you off the drugs soon enough. But ... soon enough may be too soon for me. I'm torn – between feeling dead and feeling dread. Don't know which way to turn. I know the story up to now – but I don't know how it ends. Can't even pick up my pen to write it ...

Postscript

London writer Dalton Pleasance, 33, has been named winner of the first 'Young Voices of the New Britain' award for fiction for his novel, *The Feast*, which dramatizes his year-long alcohol- and drug-riddled relationship with a disturbed fledgling young writer he attempted to mentor. He has never revealed her identity. In accepting the award and the cheque for £25,000, Mr. Pleasance expressed gratitude for the support of his wife, Portia, who recently published her first collection of short stories, *A String of Liaisons*. The couple have a one-year-old daughter, Melanie. Mr. Pleasance revealed he is writing a new novel, titled *My Month in the Country*. Reports suggest a bidding war is underway for the rights of the new book, expected to be published next Autumn.

Portia's Play

Portia ran to catch the 15:15 train that rainy Wednesday afternoon, the arms of her sweet child wrapped around her as she swept along the damp streets from the nursery to the station.

Knowing the village station's timetable by heart always came in handy.

'Mind gap, Mummy,' Melanie sang as Portia stepped into the carriage with her daughter.

'Yes, Mummy's minding,' Portia whispered in her two-year-old's ear.

As the train clicked and screeched through the half-dozen stops to their village, Portia closed her eyes, imagining her arrival.

*

Dalton: My girls are home early!
Portia: She's got a fever. The nursery called, couldn't get hold of you. I had to leave halfway through my last class. Were you out?
Dalton: No, I guess I was in the shower.
(DALTON takes MELANIE from PORTIA.)
Dalton: (to MELANIE) Let Daddy put you to bed.
Portia: I'll put the kettle on.
Dalton: (voice fades as he heads upstairs) Sorry I didn't hear the call. I'd been writing all day, with Ed Sheeran sending all his love through my headphones, then took a shower.
Portia: Not to worry, I booked off, got the earlier train. Want tea?
Dalton: Sure.
(DALTON carries MELANIE to her bedroom, kisses her then lays her down gently on her bed.)
Dalton: You go to sleep now, darling.
Melanie: Yes, Daddy. I sleeping already.
Dalton: Good girl.

*

When they arrived home, Portia saw Dalton scrambling into his best blue jeans and his ancient red football shirt. She heard the downstairs toilet flushing, then saw Dalton's colleague Iona emerge, yawning and fluffing her thick mane of red hair.

'Oh, fuck,' Iona sputtered.

"Yes, the wife and sick child came home early. Fucking inconvenient,' Portia barked.

Then she turned around with Melanie still wrapped around her neck and ran out the door, back towards the station to catch the 16:01, which took her two stops to her mother's elegant riverside flat near the shops and galleries the retired doctor loved.

*

Portia's book of short stories, *A String of Liaisons*, hadn't sold well. She had begun writing a play about Brexit called *Brit Again* but had been struggling to get past the first act. When an old friend offered her a temporary part-time job teaching secondary school English last term, she agreed.

It took some time, but Dalton came around, arranging his college classes for mornings and writing at home in the afternoons. Lately, Portia had been taking Melanie to the nursery near her school on Wednesdays. Melanie needed more time with other children and, as it turned out, Melanie loved Wednesdays at the nursery.

'Today play day, Mummy,' she'd say on Wednesday mornings.

Dalton had won a big prize for his first novel, a thinly veiled tale about his former lover, Rebecca. It landed him a second book deal and a job teaching Creative Writing at the college, a short hike from their flat, along the creek that flowed through their village dotted with hairdressers, estate agents, restaurants and a dilapidated bookshop. He had finished his second book but there had been a change in editors and his book was, as he was often wont to put it, 'being re-written for the illiterate.'

Literature had brought Portia and Dalton together, but at times it had also threatened to tear them apart. They became lovers when he was her tutor while she was finishing her Masters; he was writing his doctoral thesis on the trials of editing David Foster Wallace.

For Portia, writing offered an opportunity to reshape her family narrative, edit the part where her father ran off with a much younger woman, leaving her mother embittered and Portia bedridden with grief. Her writing helped reframe the story. Still, there were tensions. Rebecca, Dalton's old flame, had tried to lure him back into a literary tryst, have him edit the book she said she was writing from her mental health treatment centre. He never answered her request, but it caused weeks of screaming dialogue.

*

Approaching her mother's flash flat located near Tate Modern, Portia felt the warmth of Melanie's fever against her chest. The scene kept playing over and over in her head, crying out for a rewrite – Iona brazenly emerging from their downstairs washroom, her red hair looking like it had been mussed by a wild coastal wind. Portia fought off tears of exhaustion and anger. She closed her eyes, picturing another kind of homecoming.

*

Mother: What a pleasant surprise! What brings you on play day?
Portia: Mum, we need a place to crash. Dalton is home fucking Iona.
*   Melanie has a fever. And I am desperate to splash into a bath*
*   or a whisky.*
Melanie: Don't cry, Mummy.
Mother: Oh, my darlings, come in. Let me put the little one to bed.
*   I'll run you a bath while I'm up there. Put the kettle on.*
Portia: Thanks, Mum.
Mother: This too shall pass.
Portia: I hope so.

*

When they arrived, Portia just watched as her mother pulled Melanie from her arms and carried the child upstairs for a quick cool bath. Portia flopped on to the settee and a little while later her mother came back downstairs.

'I gave her some children's aspirin, put her in the spare bedroom with Wee Bunny,' she said.

The doctor poured Portia a fair swallow of golden whisky, made herself a cup of tea, then declared in her clipped professional tone, 'If this is Dalton dallying again, you need to remove yourself from the situation. Don't delay this time. If you don't leave, you won't get sympathy from me. We've been through this too often. If you leave, I will do everything I can to help. Do you hear me?'

Portia nodded, swallowed another mouthful of whisky and headed up to the bath, the sound of the 17:54 train clicking eerily in the distance.

When Portia dragged herself down to her mother's kitchen the next morning, well past time to head to class, Melanie was playing with Wee Bunny, tossing it into the air and heading it like a football towards her grandmother's second cup of tea, which was resting precariously on the arm of her easy chair.

'Mummy, me better,' Melanie said. 'When Daddy coming? I miss Daddy. Love Daddy.'

Before Portia could reply, her mother began, 'I called your school. You officially have the flu. If I were still working, I'd be struck off. However, you're not fit to face teenagers raging with hormones who have no interest in the intricacies of the bard's dialogue in *Much Ado About Nothing*.'

Portia, dressed in oversized pyjamas, her brown hair askew looked up to take in her mother's stark 'God you're hopeless' grimace. Her mother shook her head, sipped her black tea, and said dryly, 'The husband called.'

Is that how you looked at Daddy? Portia thought. *Look what happened to him. Took the train to God knows where.* She poured herself some orange juice, then climbed the stairs back to bed, punching Dalton's number into her phone before pulling the silk sheet up over her head.

After talking on the phone, Portia fell asleep, waking at one point in the middle of her slumber as her mother came and deposited a weary Melanie and a rumpled Wee Bunny beside her. Portia opened her eyes long enough to glimpse her mother looking down on them disdainfully as they snuggled together.

'I have tea with the ladies at Tate Modern, then jazz in Soho. We'll talk later,' she said.

Portia woke again an hour later when Melanie poked her in

the ribcage. Melanie wanted to play and sing, and Portia tried to forget why they were at her mother's home. They sang along to 'Galway Girl' on Portia's phone before grabbing their clothes and making for home on the 17:12. It was on time as usual.

Dalton had been full of apologies on the phone earlier. It was a stupid mistake. It would never happen again. He begged Portia to come back. He was dying to see Melanie. Never again, he vowed, telling Portia he was crossing his heart on his red football shirt. *Shit*, she thought. On that, at least, we agree. *Never again.*

On the cramped train, Portia held Melanie close, feeling the child's warm affection though suddenly wary it could take her breath away. Portia closed her eyes, wondering.

*

Dalton: (slurring) I know I said come home but I now know I need time on my own.
Portia: Time on your own, my arse.
Dalton: Come on, I'm stressed about my booker (sic)...
Portia: This has nothing to do with that piece of shit.
Dalton: Don't fucking start that shrift (sic) again...
Portia: How much have you had to drink?
Dalton: Stick to the topic.
Portia: Your book? Or your fucking around?
Dalton: I'm not making excuses.
Portia: Funny thing is, I'm not accepting any.
Dalton: Good, come give us a hug.
(PORTIA turns away then DALTON reaches towards MELANIE.)
Dalton: Give Daddy a hug.
Portia: No, she's staying right here until we finish this.
Dalton: We're already finished.
Melanie: I want a hug.
Portia: Bastard.

*

Dalton was seated at the kitchen table with his laptop in front of him but staring into space when Portia opened the front door. He got up from his chair and went to her.

'I'm sorry,' he whispered.

'I can't talk about this now. Melanie needs a bath and a change of clothes.'

'I'll do it.'

'I'm putting the kettle on.'

'Good.'

*

Melanie was so many things to Portia. Before entering the world, wrinkled and weary looking, she was a mistake, a miscalculation; then a domestic debate that inevitably included her medically minded mother; finally, an acceptance, a bundle of bliss amid the stress of marriage, work, compromise. Melanie was also a gilt-edged guarantee that Dalton would stay in the bosom of the family. A rewrite.

There was only one kind of creation Portia or Dalton understood – or had time for – before their daughter was born: words, shaped into stories, characters, plot, drama, tension, resolution. Dalton agreed to having the child because he presumed Portia would drop her writing, be a full-time mother. Done and dusted. Back to the blank page. He never said this, but Portia knew it, not just because her mother spelled it out so often in her prosaic prose.

'He's got you right where he wants you. Tied to the child.'

Portia's mother's mantra was difficult to delete from the revised manuscript she was trying to write for her life, especially since it was rooted in their family story. The respected doctor had to quit her plans to specialize in paediatrics when Portia's father left home, his young legal assistant in tow. The doctor never forgave him, editing him out of her life – and Portia's.

Was it different with Dalton? He doted on Melanie, often more than Portia did, taking her and Wee Bunny on walking tours of the neighbourhood punctuated by songs he made up to the tunes he played on his mobile phone.

That was before Wee Bunny was left at Nana's after an earlier separation precipitated by Dalton's constant 'lunches' with Jen, a bar maid in the village. Or was she Jan? Portia couldn't properly read the miniscule script above her left breast that afternoon when she stopped for coffee, and to see what she was up against, or rather who she was up against. *How could he? A bar maid yet!*

Now, post-Iona (she had to believe this), Portia felt like she was riding on two different tracks around the city. Dalton was doing well in the rewriting of the book, rarely complained about the new editor, spent afternoons with Melanie so Portia could get back to *Brit Again* when she wasn't teaching. He even tried to get along with Portia's mother (that was remarkable), remembered Portia's birthday, bought red roses and a romantic card from the village flower shop.

However, Portia couldn't let herself believe that her life would continue to play out like that. It never did.

At the end of term, Portia took the 12:01 to meet her mother for lunch before her interview at the school. They were willing to offer her more hours the following September. Portia felt torn. Her Brexit play was coming along. Finally, the dialogue was sharp, punchy. Getting to the heart of the separation. Still, she could use the money the teaching brought.

She closed her weary eyes.

*

Mother: Isn't it time you gave up this writing... thing?
Portia: Writing keeps me alive, but, you're right, we need the money.
    Teaching pays. And then there's Melanie.
Mother: And then there's Melanie?
Portia: You know what I mean.
Mother: Do I?
Portia: Mother, please. I need your support here.
Mother: Where's Dalton in all this?
Portia: He's fine with whatever at the moment.
Mother: Hmm.
Portia: What are you suggesting?
Mother: Just make sure you read the situation closely.
Portia: He's turned a new page.
Mother: Okay.

*

The restaurant was quiet save the occasional clink of cutlery. Portia's mother was seated in a corner when Portia arrived for lunch, her eyes fixed on the leather-bound menu, though she could certainly recite it by heart if asked to.

'Am I late?' Portia asked.

'No.'

'Good, but Mother, are you okay?'

'I am.'

'I'm starving.'

'I think I will just sip this for now.'

'You don't look happy, Mother.'

'I'm fine.'

'Okay.'

'However, I have a question.'

'What is it?'

'Tell me, what does this Iona look like?'

'Why do you ask?'

'Well.'

'No, Mother.'

'What does she look like, Portia?'

'Red hair... You saw her? *Them?*'

Portia took a sip of water from the crystal glass in front of her, put the glass down and brought her hands together as if to pray.

Her mother waited a long moment, then spoke, pausing between each word, as if adding a full stop.

'Darling, you do know that clinging to Dalton won't bring Daddy back, don't you?'

'For God's sake, Mother.'

'That you're making a fool of yourself staying with that man because you want to fix Daddy leaving when you were two years old. It's textbook, Portia. But it won't work. Trust me.'

'It's too late for that.'

'Okay, but don't you know that this cannot continue? It will kill you.'

Portia began to cry. Her mother handed her a tissue.

'No, but you're the fucking doctor, mother, so tell me.'

However, Portia had heard enough words. She got up and left the table, ran from the restaurant and caught the 12:40 to school, closing her eyes for a moment on the train.

*

(PORTIA lies in her pink bedroom clutching her favourite stuffed rabbit, listening to MOTHER and FATHER yell at each other while FATHER packs his suitcase. PORTIA tries to hold back her tears.)
Father: Be quiet or you'll upset the child.
Mother: Who will upset the child?
Father: Just lower your voice.
Mother: Why should I?
Father: She's very sensitive.
Mother: She's upset because you're leaving, you bastard. What the fuck do you think you're doing, leaving with that ridiculous hussy? Honestly, how long do you think that will last?
Father: Who knows? But it will be lovely while it does last. That's for certain.
Mother: Listen to yourself! You disgust me.
Father: I suppose I always have.
Mother: Just get the fuck out.

*

After the interview, in which she was offered the job but declined it, Portia went to her desk for the last time and typed out the final scene she had been working on for many weeks, hoping to get it right. She wanted an ending that made sense. She thought about what her mother had said, about her father's leaving, about Dalton, about Melanie, dear Melanie. Then about Dalton and Melanie. Then she ran for the 15:15, never crowded, always on time.

That evening, the doorbell rang and Dalton, who had been playing with Melanie and Wee Bunny, got up to respond.

*

(DALTON answers the door wearing his best jeans and a scruffy red football shirt.)

Met Officer: Dalton Pleasance?

Dalton: *(laughs nervously)* Yes.

Met Officer: I'm sorry to inform you there's been an incident at the station involving your wife. I'm afraid she's ...

(A train clicks by in the distance obscuring the words of the MET OFFICER then DALTON gasps in horror.)

Melanie: *(from the other room)* Come on, Daddy, it's play day.

(MET OFFICER leaves.)

Melanie: *(running to DALTON, who is staring out the door as the MET OFFICER departs)* Is it still play day, Daddy? I love play day.

Dalton: *(crying, turns back to MELANIE, whispers)* Yes, darling, it's play day.

END

Franny Falls in Love

❧

Franny had a lunch date.

First time in ages.

Once bitten . . .

She stayed up half the night worrying about it. Gave herself a bit of a headache. Not a migraine, mind, but verging on one. Lying in bed next morning, she thought about cancelling the date. Looked at her phone – one more time. He hadn't changed his mind. At least it seemed that way. *What the hell, might as well go*, she thought.

Why meet me at the station? Must be from out of town. Up north? Oh, God. What have I got myself into?

Not again.

She pulled the hood of her grey raincoat up over her aching head to ward off the February wind and snow as she darted for the train station in the heart of the village. He said he'd meet her there at noon. *Said* he would. *Fat chance,* she thought. *Still, I might as well get out and about for a change.*

So, what's this now – snow! Bloody hell. In bleeding England? Once every winter, I figure.

Franny's ancient trainers were leaking, and her thin socks were already soaked. *Could be one devil of a date*, she mused. She ducked into the heated station waiting area to get out of the wintry weather. *Love this country.*

She shook the melting snowflakes off her raincoat, jeans and trainers, catching a glimpse of herself reflected in the waiting room window. It looked like she was dancing the way she had with her best friend Grace at O'Neill's bar on the village high street that Saturday night a few years back.

God, she missed those days.

Missed Grace, to be more accurate. Missed her badly.

'Gracie, come back,' she whispered as though she was praying. 'Please.'

Then she stopped, stared, like that mammoth General Wolfe statue in Greenwich Park that she loved so much, the one that glares triumphantly across the Thames. However, what she had in her sights just then were two elderly women and an odd-looking gentleman with a blue flat cap and white straggly beard. They were all rifling through three sagging wooden shelves of battered books, stuffing them into their big fat bags and his deep coat pockets as if the storm outside was going to keep them in hibernation – for weeks. Franny must have missed that weather bulletin. *Better check it out.*

Readers! For God's sake!

'What the actual fuck,' she said to no one – though the old ladies certainly heard her, momentarily raising their fuzzy winter hats and white eyebrows in her direction. The old man paid no heed. Must have been deaf, kept fingering the ancient paperbacks, muttering to himself.

Franny stopped herself mid-rant because she could hear Grace telling her that that kind of language was 'not very polite, not very Christian, Franny'. Grace had always been more of a churchgoing and God-fearing kind of girl than Franny. They first met at Sunday school when they were just gangly and gabby five-year olds. *Was always more churchgoing.* That's changed, but Franny could still hear Grace chiding her and so she stopped her expletive-filled wondering aloud and just stared at the goings-on in the waiting room, whispering, 'What's this? A library at the Blackheath train station! Welcome to the twenty-first century ... I guess.'

She laughed out loud.

Ever since her best friend Grace left for America, after what Franny and Grace had quietly begun to call the *incident,* Franny had felt lost. It was like her left hand was missing. Or, some other part of her, something like that. She could never quite express that sort of thing. Not like Grace. Grace could always say things like they were written down in a book or something.

Franny still received texts now and then from Grace, but Grace had started business school in America – New York City, where her mum and her mum's new man, Warner, settled – that was after Grace's mum's divorce and everything. Grace never talked much about that. Warner's American. So off they went. Then Grace joined them.

Some days Franny hasn't been able to reconcile the fact that

Grace is gone, but she was at least starting to accept that since Grace had begun getting on with her own life after that awful *incident* – in a whole different country, studying business, maybe someday even setting up a whole chain of fancy nail-varnishing shops – maybe Franny ought to be getting out and about too.

Still, Grace in New York? The Empire State Building! Franny could barely imagine it. She just shook her head whenever she thought about it.

Where am I? Still here.

That's part of what this date was all about. Moving on.

But there was still no sign of the fellow, so Franny decided to dig into the library. *What the hell,* she thought. She grabbed a book off the top shelf, a thin volume called *A String of Liaisons*, short stories by some frighteningly thin young woman who used to live in the village, where Franny has spent her whole life. At least that's what the back cover told her. Funny, Franny had never met her. *Anyways,* she thought, *I'll see what it's all about. Sounds sexy.*

Franny unzipped her rucksack and tossed the paperback into the bag Grace gave her for her birthday two years ago, bright red with pink stars plastered all over it. Grace knew Franny's style.

The book settled next to her water bottle, phone charger and makeup bag. Maybe she'd look at it later. Possibly bring it back if it didn't interest her.

Books.

Grace used to tell her she needed to read more books, improve her mind, get ahead, but Franny never seemed to have time for books; she was always glued to her phone.

She checked her email and texts again – the third time since leaving her flat. No messages from her so-called date. *Nothing. Bugger.* She wandered out onto the damp platform. *Another dreary day,* she thought. The snow had settled into a more familiar rain, but the wind was still bitter. No sign of this man who looked so good on the dating site, blond and brooding, with one earring and a wisp of a beard. There was not much sign of life at all at the station. Must be that virus. Everybody was staying home, Franny thought.

Franny was a bit unwell herself, felt like spitting out the bitter tang in her mouth. She'd been tasting it all morning. It was like some kind of toxic cocktail of blood and tears, probably brought on by her night of insomnia, YouTube, a mammoth bag of crisps washed down with cheap white wine from the all-night shop. The women's WC at the station was locked, for some reason. *Hell*, she thought. She was about to spit onto the tracks but stopped herself. *Shit. Grace would have had a fit.*

Grace. How she missed that girl.

Franny pulled the water bottle from her rucksack and gulped down a couple of mouthfuls, turned to leave the station – then saw him. Not the date. She'd already forgotten that bastard, who she only knew as Oliver99 from the Red Top online dating service – he of 'no fixed address, no current commitments, no long-term plans, just out for a good time'. *Yeah, right.* Forgotten him totally.

No, another him. Maybe even Him. *God*, she thought, *you should see this guy, Gracie!*

He was at least six feet tall with a small scar near his right eye, long brown hair in a kind of seventies wave, a slight slouch, a long leather jacket, and dark Nordic eyes. Very dark. She just knew he was from that part of the world. Of course, he also had a young blonde woman next to him – in fact, glued to him, like a third arm or something.

No matter.

He carried a bundle of books under his arm, hardbacks that clearly had not come from the station library. He wandered into the little library, gave the three shelves of books a cursory glance, shook his head, frowned, turned and went out onto the station platform. It looked like he and the attached young woman were headed to the city.

Franny sighed. *That man has just got to be an actor or something, maybe a movie star, a director, famous.*

Handsome too.

'Maybe I do need to read more,' she muttered under her breath as she eyed his bundle of books.

Franny thought she might just be in love.

Not that again.

Forget the date.

Franny took out her Oyster card, touched in and got on the same carriage as the couple. She sat nearby, kept her eye on them. The young blonde woman managed to get even closer to him, snuggling in, as they sat down together. He opened a fat hardback book, put on his fashionable specs and began to read. The book looked dead serious to Franny, thick with a red ribbon bookmark. He was lost in it. She couldn't take her eyes off him. It was like she was watching a wild animal in its natural habitat. At peace, yet ready to pounce. Beautiful. His companion, her of the blonde hair, pink nails and high heels, flipped open her phone and started moving her thumbs rapidly back and forth across the keyboard.

Soon the rumble of the train put Franny to sleep. The train always put Franny to sleep. Especially when she had had a bad night. And Franny had had a very disturbed night. Not the worst, but bad enough. When she woke up three stations later, they were gone. *He* was gone.

Shit.

Franny got off the train at the next station and found another train to take her back to the village.

She was fighting a migraine – and she was dateless.

Trying to stay awake on the train, Franny reached into her rucksack and pulled out the book from the station library …

Liaisons.

She settled in and began to read – for the first time in ages.

*

When they were seven years old, Franny and Grace decided to run away together. On the Saturday morning at the beginning of half-term, Grace made peanut butter and jam sandwiches in her family's kitchen overlooking the car park of the council estate; two flights above her, Franny filled an old Thermos of her dad's with apple juice, and took a couple of ripe bananas from the fruit bowl her mother kept replenishing in the tiny dining area of their flat. They met in the car park at eight o'clock before their parents were up, and off they went.

Where? Franny couldn't really remember despite all the plans they had made after school on Friday, so she didn't really know, but Grace had a plan. Franny bit her lip.

'Take my hand, Franny,' Grace said, as they headed towards the centre of the village.

'You're safe with me. I know how to get us there.'

'Where are we going again, Gracie?'

'Tower of London.'

'What's "Tower of London" again?'

'I'll show you. It's like a big old jail or something. They have the Queen's jewels there.'

'Then what are we going to do?'

'Go on a boat ride to New York City.'

'Empire State Building!'

'That's right.'

Grace took Franny's hand and they headed out of the council estate through the littered car park, to the centre of the village. They passed the train station, crossed carefully at the traffic lights, then, after another set of lights, headed out across the heath, glancing up at the grand church where Grace's parents went every Sunday. Soon they were in the park, walking quickly, glancing behind them every few minutes. They stopped and stood a long moment gazing up at the statue of General Wolfe before heading down the steep hill towards the River Thames.

They were on their way.

Then it started to rain. Within minutes the girls were soaked right through to the skin. Franny started to cry. Franny huddled under Grace's raincoat. They found a dry spot under a big old tree near the gates. There was a coffee shop nearby, but when Grace ran out into the rain and tried the door, she found it was locked. The two girls then sat under the tree and tried to dry themselves.

'I want to go home,' Franny said.

'Let's see if the rain stops.'

'It won't.'

'Look, the sun is coming out.'

'It's still raining.'

'Just a bit.'

'I'm cold.'

'Don't forget – Empire State Building!' Grace said.

Franny wasn't just wet and tired. She missed her mum. She answered: 'I want to go home.'

Grace just frowned, got out their peanut butter and jam sandwiches, gave one to Franny, then they munched quietly, watching the tree branches bend with the wind. The rain continued, coming in waves at times, then died down again.

They sipped their apple juice for a little while then ate the bananas, and when the rain stopped for a moment, Grace asked Franny, 'Should we keep going, at least to the Tower of London? The Queen's jewels!'

'You go on. I want to go home. I'm wet and cold.'

'Do you know the way home?'

Franny just bit her bottom lip until it hurt.

'Come on, give me your hand. I'll take you,' Grace said.

'Where?'

'Home.'

Franny started crying again. Then she took Grace's wet hand.

'Love you, Gracie.'

'I know.'

*

Franny stayed at home for a few days after following that handsome man on to the train.

I must be mad, she thought. Acting like a stalker and all. She laughed at herself. Then she settled under the thin grey blanket on her well-worn settee, shook her head, sipped her tea and began the second story in *Liaisons*.

'I'm self-isolating,' she muttered to her black-and-white cat, Troll. 'Move over. Make room,' She kicked out at him gently.

Troll jumped off the settee, gave her a look, then disappeared.

Franny's flat was a tiny studio on the edge of the village. She worked part-time (whenever they called her) in the village bakery, baking scones in the morning and serving the hungry lunchtime crowd. However, she never made enough to get out of that flat and into a decent one with an actual bedroom. Luxury. She moved out of her parents' little house after they caught her smoking weed in her bedroom – for the fifth time, that was. It was rough financially, but she wanted to be on her own. She and Grace used to talk about moving in together when Grace was working in the village nail salon, but when Grace lost that job, she decided to stay at home.

That all changed after the *incident*, and then Grace moved to America, where she had her own tiny apartment in her mum and Warner's house. Franny found her studio flat in the village, but it took forever, and things were tense at home during the long delay. Even then, the landlord warned her the rent would rise after a few months. Franny still hadn't figured out how she was going to cope with that. The bakery said they couldn't afford to offer her any more hours – what with the virus and all, she was lucky to have any.

And it could get worse.

Franny fell asleep after reading the second story in *Liaisons*, a tale about a girl falling in lust with an artist who had been dead for half a century. Strange little story, but she couldn't resist, reading rapidly, turning page after page. Franny woke up several hours later. The flat was shrouded in darkness and Troll was nowhere to be seen. *He'll be back*, she thought. She picked up her book again and read the next six stories right through.

'God, that girl knows nothing about sex,' she said to the bare walls, looking around for Troll. 'Then again, what the hell do I know about sex these days? Nothing. That's for sure.'

She got out her phone and checked to see if there any new messages from Oliver99. Nothing. *Men! What the hell is with them, anyway?*

Franny grabbed a stale scone and a glass of orange juice, swallowed them quickly then pulled on her trainers, jeans and a T-shirt. She called Troll, to no avail, stuffed *Liaisons* into her rucksack, grabbed her keys and headed out the door of her flat.

'Hey Gracie, I'm going to the bloody library,' she laughed to herself as she made her way toward the station in rare resplendent sunshine.

Franny picked through the library shelves, resting her hand a little longer on a thick book called *My Month in the Country*. She read the blurb on the back and was about to return it to the shelf – too many posh people spending their time in landscaped gardens, she thought – but she was intrigued by the cover, a gorgeous country house down a tree-lined lane with a big old mutt wandering its way toward the mansion. It reminded her of one of her secondary school texts, Thomas Hardy or D. H. Lawrence, one of those blokes she never did finish reading. She could hear Grace giving her stick over that. Still, she always loved the arty covers, wanted to go to those places in the shires one day herself.

Her and Grace, that was.

'I'd like a bit of that,' she said to herself, looking at the cover of *My Month in the Country* again. 'I'll grab it,' she added a moment later. 'Oh my God, Gracie, they've got me reading.'

Heading out of the waiting room, stuffing the book into her rucksack as she went, Franny bumped into a young girl with stringy light brown hair, who was holding the hand of a tall man in a leather coat, carrying – Oh God – another bundle of hardback books.

Nordic eyes.

Franny dropped her book, swore out loud then quickly covered her mouth, picked up her book and said, 'God, sorry, sorry. I didn't see you coming ... I ... never mind.'

The young girl frowned vaguely in Franny's direction, then turned away, but the man – *the man* – smiled, bowed like he was in some old period film, and then they moved past Franny towards the bookshelves.

Out on the platform, Franny found a vacant bench, sat down, closed her eyes, took a deep breath and whispered, 'What a fool I am. I must be losing my mind. Throwing my book all over the station. God. He's got a girlfriend. He's got a daughter. Hell, he's probably got a life.'

She shook her head, fought off a few miserable tears, pulled out a tissue and wiped her eyes, then her nose. She got out her phone and sent Grace a text: *Gracie, it's me again. Would love to talk when you can. Miss you madly. Franny.*

Then she checked the time and realized Grace was more than likely in class. *Of course, she was. What a fool I am. Another text she can't answer.*

She took out her new book and flipped through the chapters, wondering if it was just too many pages, before returning to the opening chapter. She stopped and read.

I had hoped that my month in God's green country would give me rest, respite, relaxation, so that I might return to the grim work of running my struggling little publishing company in this nondescript borough of damp old London, fully restored. However, it did none of that. In fact, my month in the country nearly killed me.

'Oh God,' Franny muttered. 'I'm not sure this is for me just now.'

However, she shook her head and threw the book into the rucksack, got up and headed home.

No Nordic eyes in sight.

Sadly.

*

After secondary school, Franny went to college to study catering and hospitality. Her mum and dad had wanted her to just get a job, help the family out financially. Her dad had lost his job in the pub and her mum worked only part-time in a betting shop. Things were tough. Franny listened to her parents, but she had been spending a lot of time with Grace, and Grace was going to college to study business, accounting and law.

'Education, Franny. You need education or you'll just end

up in low-end jobs and council flats like our parents. I'm going to college. You can come too. You're smart, girl.'

'No, I'm not.'

'Yeah, you are. You just need to convince yourself of that. Your grades are okay.'

'Barely.'

'I'm sure you can do it, girl. Bit of hard work won't kill you. Come on, let's go check it out.'

'I got to wash my hair.'

'Your hair's fine, Franny.'

'No, it's shit.'

'Okay, true, but it doesn't matter.'

'I don't know how you do it, Gracie, but you got me. Once more time. I'm coming. Don't tell my mum. Not yet.'

'Okay, we'll surprise her.'

'God.'

So, Franny enrolled at college – and worked weekends at the bakery in the village, trying to keep everybody happy.

It didn't last.

On her first day at college Franny went to the cafeteria at lunchtime and was inching along in the queue for coffee and a tuna sandwich and kept getting kicked on the back of her trainers by a big bloke in a red football shirt. She turned around to tell him off, looked up but saw that his eyes were fixed on his phone. Franny shook her head. *No point in talking to him.*

She turned back around and began moving forward again, and again the fellow kicked her left trainer. Franny turned around, furious, but this time she was met with a wide grin and a 'gotcha' finger pointing at her.

'Hey, Franny, don't you remember me? Sunday school? Back in the day? You and that black girl... Gracie, always hushing me when the teacher was telling us about Jesus? Come on, girl, chill.'

'Dougie?'

'Still me.'

'What the...'

They took their lunches outside and sat under a great old maple tree and caught up, laughed a lot. Dougie and his family had moved up north, but he had come back to the area for college. He was studying IT and computing.

Franny kept her eye out for Grace, though her schedule was different from Franny's, and she didn't expect to see her. Grace had never liked Dougie when they were kids. She would have been warning Franny off.

Of course, she would.

A few days later, Dougie took Franny back to his tiny flat in the basement of an old house near the college and they smoked weed, had sex on his lumpy single bed, fell asleep, woke up and tried to do it again but gave up and lit up instead.

Franny kept going to her morning classes but every afternoon she grabbed a sandwich in the cafeteria with Dougie and went back to his place. That was the pattern for the whole first term. Her grades were not good. Her parents yelled at her when she came home late one Monday afternoon smelling like weed. Franny wanted to move out but couldn't afford to.

Her mum called Grace and the next day Grace showed up in the cafeteria, grabbed Franny by the hand and took her to a tiny café a few blocks from school. Dougie kept pinging Franny on her phone, but Grace took it and put it in her bag.

'I'll give your phone back when we've had lunch – and a talk.'

'Talk! Sounds serious, girl.'

'Up to you.'

'Are you suddenly smoking weed again?'

'Maybe. What of it?'

'It's your life, girl.'

'Yeah, it is.'

'You going to class?'

'Maybe.'

'Not good enough.'

'Look, Gracie, me and Dougie are just having a laugh.'

'You love that boy?'

'I dunno, we're just ... Maybe I do, I'm trying to figure that out.'

'Screwing up your chance to make something of yourself. That's what.'

Franny had no answer. Her eyes started to fill with tears. She went off to the washroom, cleaned herself up, and when she came back, said to Grace, 'I'm not smart like you, Gracie, not pretty like you. Dougie's okay, he likes me. I like him, maybe even love him.'

'Uh huh. He doesn't love you or he wouldn't keep you out of class every afternoon.'

'You never did like him.'

'You're right about that. Always was a bit too stuck on himself, even when he was a kid.'

'I don't know.'

Grace put down her coffee cup. 'Just show yourself more respect, girl. You like him, okay. See him. But go to school, read your schoolbooks, get ahead. Stay off the weed.'

'You sound like my mum.'

'I'm not *that* old, girl.'

*

Franny arrived back in her flat to find Troll scratching at the coffee-stained arm of her settee again. She shooed him away, dropped her rucksack onto the settee, pulled out *My Month in the Country* and began reading. *Posh, she thought, but okay. There's something here. I've got to figure out what it is.* And she kept reading.

She got a couple of hours work at the village bakery the next morning, but after her shift the manager told that was it, that the virus was killing sales and that she wouldn't be calling her back any time soon.

Shit.

Franny would need to hit her parents up for a small loan, and they were skint as well. She went home, made herself a coffee and a slice of toast and peanut butter, and snuggled up with Troll and dipped into *A Month in the Country*. She had to get away from her life. The book would do it.

Franny hadn't heard back from Grace but was trying not to get too pissed off because she knew Grace was working hard at her business studies. She checked her phone often. No message from Grace. No Oliver99. Nothing.

She took a long hot bath, cleaned up her flat like they were telling everybody on television to do because of that virus, got rid of Troll's litter then settled in for a few more chapters of her book. She was hooked. Gracie would be proud of her, ten chapters. *Not sure what the Hell it is all about yet but that girl in that big house sure knows how to tell her man off. She rules. Love that.*

She laughed out loud.

Franny took her book to bed and read half the night, speeding through the last chapter just before the sun came up. She closed her eyes and tried to sleep, wondering, *How the Hell does that guy know all that stuff about gardens back then? Probably Gracie would say, "He read a lot of books to create that book."*

She laughed out loud..

Of course, she'd say that. Probably right, too.

Then Franny went to sleep, slept half the day.

Franny only woke up when Troll had headbutted her on her shoulder. Troll was hungry. Franny was starving too. She fed Troll, then toasted a cinnamon raisin bagel for herself, slathering on the butter as if a famine was coming after the virus. *God, I needed that,* she thought.

She grabbed her big fat book and threw it in her rucksack and headed out to the station. *Never mind weed, I think I've got a whole new drug here. Wait 'til Gracie finds out.*

The station was dead quiet. She had the little library in the waiting room all to herself. She put *My Month in the Country* on the top shelf and, this time, spent a good fifteen minutes looking more carefully at the selection. She burst out laughing as her eye caught sight of a thick paperback, *Franny and Zooey*.

'Should be *Franny and Gracie*,' she laughed. She turned to the back cover and began to read about the reclusive American writer, then she heard a deep guttural voice behind her.

'Are you certain you want to read that bit of trash? I thought you were a much more serious reader than that. Every time I come to this little library you're here.'

She turned around.

Nordic eyes.

Definitely, Nordic eyes.

'God, I don't know. I was only … Look, I'm just getting back into reading.'

'May I suggest a book for you, then? You might love it.'

'Why? I mean, why not? Sure. Yes.'

Very tall, she thought. *But is he laughing at me, or just smiling? I never know.*

She stood aside so that he (*he*) could get to the bookshelves. Instead, he just stuck his hand out, then quickly withdrew it and offered Franny his elbow instead. The virus, of course.

They both laughed.

'By the way, I'm Karl,' he said. 'Nice to make your acquaintance.'

'Franny, well … like the book.'

Karl threw his head back and laughed 'I get it – *Franny and Zooey*.'

Franny felt flush, wondered if she was getting the virus.

'Yeah, I don't think it's for me, however.'

'Try this little volume,' he said, pulling a thick hardback out of his black leather man bag, opening it up, scribbling something quickly on the first page in pencil and handing it to Franny.

She looked down at his scrawl for a long time but couldn't make out the words. Maybe they were in a foreign language. She then turned to the back cover of the book and saw the author's photo.

God. It was him. Karl. Nordic eyes.

She looked up to thank him, but he was gone.

*

Franny had tried to convince Grace to go to the police after the *incident*. It was one of the few times she ever got angry with her friend. It didn't last. After Grace stood up in front of the church full of godly folks and told them about being raped by the church elder, she needed a place to crash. She went to Franny's tiny flat.

Even though Grace was silent and sombre, and spent most of the time in bed, sipping tea and taking bits of toast Franny brought for her, it was one of Franny's favourite times. She wasn't sure why exactly.

Taking care of Grace, maybe. That was quite a change.

That thought only came to her a long time after, though.

When Grace moved to New York to study business, Franny quit school, started missing shifts at the bakery, started smoking weed again. Dougie had dumped her for some skinny little thing in first year, but she called him up. No response. No surprise.

Grace had been right about Dougie.

*

Franny got home, kicked Troll off the settee and opened up her new book, *A Man in Love*. She began to read.

Then her phone rang, and it was Grace, calling from New York.

'Girl, what's happening? Are you in love or something? All those texts. What's his name? What's he look like? Handsome, I bet.'

Clutching her new book – the one with Nordic eyes on the back cover, Franny cried out like she was speaking across an ocean without the use of her phone. 'Gracie, I miss you, girl. Yes, I think I'm in love. In a way, I guess. I don't know ... Let me tell you the story.'

Time Enough for Sadness

Denial

I hear foxes fornicating at four in the morning, huffing and puffing, shrieking; there's a low, soft moan, then a deadly silence.

Another disturbed night. Hope they leave my yellow nasturtiums and the new-fangled irrigation system alone this time.

I fall sleep again an hour later, just as those morning warblers begin to sing out of tune in the zen garden. I dream of moving on from the man, making my way, 'evolving', as my grizzled counsellor, Derek, calls it.

Now, awake again, at a slightly more reasonable hour. Sunlight is streaking in through gaps in the pink blinds, a new addition to my nesting place to allow me a little longer to enjoy my solitary mornings.

There are too many issues to deal with today: a sermon to write for my diminishing congregation (on forgiveness, I'm still having trouble with that); a difficult meeting with my curate, Tom (too orthodox); Group (sod them all); the note from my GP (she wants me to make an appointment – bloody headaches); the tree surgeon (that old maple's poorly, its yellow leaves wilting and curling).

Since Peter's been gone, I have created a mini kitchen up here in what was once our bedroom. It helps me ease into the day. I have a small kettle, a black-and-white M&S tin stuffed with Orange Pekoe tea bags, a small fridge with a spot of milk, and a couple of croissants from the village bakery tucked up in what was my Mum's tatty kitchen bread bin.

Then I sip my tea, feel the sweet chocolate croissant on my tongue liquefy and slowly make its way down to my growling tummy. I look across the brightening off-white bedroom and consider my half-century-old body, both visible and covered parts: legs, long enough and with some decent muscle tone, though my knobby knees have gotten worse with age and look more like goose bumps; stomach, well, I need to get the exercise bike out of the garage; breasts, once described as 'parfait' by him, now broadening but still with life in them, I think; bottom, never mind; face, like my Mum's, still not bad though; hair, a greying frazzled mess – time for Zac, the hairdresser. Add it all up? It's me. Though it's not really me, just what others see. Nothing I can do to change that. Such is life, this side of the grave.

One more cuppa. Then I can face the day.

Out of bed.

Downstairs, one step at a time.

I draw the blinds to my blessed back garden.

My body collapses. I am on my knees. My face hits the floor. I hear myself scream, sob, choke. I try to get up. Fall again.

Time passes. How much, I don't know.

I am down in some kind of black hole, some kind of Hell.

Lost.

Unable to breathe.

More time.

Finally, I try to speak, but the sound I hear is not human. Ghostly.

I scream.

'No, no, no!'

'God no.'

'Peter!'

'What have you done?'

Everything goes black.

*

I loved your body. From the moment I glimpsed it amid the musty volumes of long-dead biblical scholars in our ancient seminary library. There, where I first encountered it. Encountered you. Your sleek brown hair, your scruffy beard, a touch too hippy-like for me; but those spindly legs in those faded jeans, distracting me from my search for the few feminist theologians who had managed to worm their way into this august collection, mesmerizing me as you reached for Aquinas or Augustine, one of those 'great male thinkers' you adored; your sandal-clad scrawny toes scrunching towards the stacks while I basked in my sweet thoughts about the gentle curve of your tiny blue-jeaned bottom.

'I loved what you were saying about the new feminist theologies in class the other day. It would be great to chat about it, unless you are too deep in contemplation of ...'

God, he's in my class. How did I miss that?

'Give me a minute,' I say gathering my books, notes, pen.

'Tempus fugit, scholar.'

Just two hours, two coffees, two glasses of cheap red wine later, I held your arse, guided you as you gently came inside me, again and again. I loved that body. Not just then, not just in the first blush of our sexual experience, but year after year, through dating, through engagement and after marrying. And I loved *you*. I am talking to *you* now. For so many reasons, for so many years. Even after you finally walked away, three years ago. Left me dying of thirst for your love, your spiritual love, your sexual love. Left me, a woman of substance, a well-thought-of priest. Left me, even after those months of trying to comprehend what was happening to you, reaching out, pulling you back into my warm embrace. Left me, even after I reluctantly gave you the space that you craved, even after I had welcomed you into our bed again.

Left me, taking that body.

*

Now, here it is again. Here *you* are again. How did you creep back into my home? I changed the locks. I took precautions.

Yet, there you are. Your body. The body that once enticed me, held me, loved me. That body. Now hanging from the maple tree in what was our back garden, our zen garden. Hanging there – dead. Your head cocked to one side, your face bruised purple almost beyond recognition.

I open the glass doors to the garden and puke from the stench of your death. I go back inside, shut the doors, look out at you, dead in the garden that once brought us so may hours of pure green bliss, coupled together on that sloping settee, gripping mugs of tea, gazing out the window.

*

Did I scream again?

The doorbell rings. Who called the police? Why do we need an ambulance? The fire brigade is here. So is Derek, my counsellor. Someone cut him down. Where are they taking him?

The young policeman comes over to talk to me.

'No,' I say. 'I have no idea how my ex-husband got into the garden in the middle of the night and hanged himself.'

Why would he do it? I tell him, 'I don't care.'

Of course, I care.

Is that another siren? Why are my neighbours gathering across the street?

God, you are always with me. Where the Hell are you now?

I trip over something in the kitchen. A stool? I fall to the floor and everything goes black – again.

Then I'm freezing and weeping, in a dream, I think. I have gone to the very Hell I have always assured my greying congregation doesn't exist.

I hear a voice, faint but familiar, singing some ancient melody.

> Don't look to the fated tree,
> That's not our reality.
> Look to the sky, wonder why
> Death's not our finality.

*

They must have carried me to my bed. I sleep for two days. Or stay in my bed. Drink nothing. Eat nothing. My grim young curate, wearing his bloody collar still, looks in on me, brings me tea. It sits at the bedside growing cold, like my heart.

I hate you. Yes, I am talking to *you*. I never thought I would hate you, but this... You not only killed yourself. You killed a part of me.

I hate what I am thinking. I hate my hate.

*

Days go by. Everything is hazy. Tom, my curate (I remember his name), comes and goes and leaves me tea, sandwiches, mini pizzas from the pizza parlour in the village. I pick away. My head aches.

I can still see you hanging from that tree when I look out the garden window if I venture downstairs for tea bags. Even after so many days of bitter mourning, there you are, like a shrouded blimp looming over our village as you move across the city. You couldn't just have found a tree in the middle of the deep city woods where we once tramped on our Mondays off.

What kind of wife – even ex-wife – thinks like that?

Do you remember those days we shared, wandering through brush thick with dew and dung near our first churches? They were such bliss. Even once after *that* day ...

Now this.

You were afraid no one would find you if you went deep into the woods in the city or out into the country. That's just like you. It had to be here, in what was our garden and is now my garden. Going off somewhere you wouldn't be found would have been too kind of you.

I hear Derek sighing gently, 'You know you don't really think that, you're grieving for a man you once loved. Say nothing for a while, Faith. Listen to what your God is telling you.'

Have I imagined this? I know Derek was here earlier, with my GP and my now collar-less curate, who was scurrying around making tea. I've never heard Derek talk of God before.

*

Tom wants to talk to me about the funeral, but I keep putting him off. Peter's parents died years ago in a traffic accident in America and he and his sister Lizzie, who lives on an isolated island off the southern coast of Australia, had been estranged for years. I've met her just a few times. Tom tried calling the number I had for Lizzie and it was no longer valid.

It feels like it has been many weeks now, though I am not sure. They cut you down, but you are still hanging in that tree. They took your body to the morgue, but you are still hanging in that tree. They conducted an autopsy on your bloated corpse, but you are still hanging in that tree. Tom is pushing me to hold a funeral in my crumbling church, but you are still hanging in that tree. They say it's time to put you in the ground, but you are still hanging in that tree ...

I remember when you first went off on your own, I received a phone call from some island in the South Pacific. That conversation – punctuated with cracking along the line, your tears, and mine – haunts me.

'It's Peter. Can we talk, just a few minutes? I just wanted to say—'

'Come home now and sort it out.' Peter, I want you here. I am willing to erase these past few months, all your wandering, everything.'

'You don't want me, Faith. You want your illusion of our marriage. The *before* marriage, not the *after* marriage. I don't quite know why I phoned. I guess I was checking to see that you are okay. This wandering is not just ...'

'Really, Peter. Don't—'

'I have to go.'

'Of course.'

*

I slip downstairs early one morning to get a pill for my aching head.

You are still there, haunting me with your dead eyes. You didn't hang yourself in that squat dogwood. That was too small, too fragile. That gnarly little tree would never have held your six-foot frame, all that bulk, from church suppers, apple pies baked by your good-hearted Christian women wanting to support their priest after all your visiting, your tender listening, your 'may-the-peace-of-Christ-be-with-you' hugs. Little did they know. Little did *I* know. You had stopped loving me. You had stopped loving your orthodox little congregation just across the lawn. Stopped loving your God. Stopped believing in anything but satisfying your need for sexual satisfaction, some kind of twisted revenge for the pain we'd shared years before. Took that young Sunday-school teacher with you when you decided to take a year off.

How old was she? Not so young that she didn't see through you, tossing you aside on the ferry from Auckland to Waiheke Island on your great escape. She came back here, begging forgiveness. I sent her away. She wanted cheap grace. I wanted her to share my pain.

That dogwood was your choice; subtle, you called it when we planted it. A modest bloom, just six weeks a year. Bright and beautiful, you used to say, sing, even. But the maple? That was my preference. I planted a long time ago. It's stable, full of life. It offers generous shade and fiery seasonal colour to our little plot of neutral land between your parish, St. Mary's, ancient Roman Catholic standard-bearer, and mine, St. Margaret's, a rebel Anglican parish. They remain high church and low church, the history of the Church in a nutshell. Now both churches are struggling and there is talk of amalgamating.

The garden sits between the two church properties, with an ancient wall on three sides, providing you with a quiet corner to come and die, while I slept fitfully upstairs.

I still see you, hanging there on the deeply rooted maple tree on which I based so many sermons, my tree of life, my hope each spring, my life-sustaining oxygen, and now your wooden cross. And you will always be hanging there. But yours is a self-serving sacrifice. You're no Jesus. Just a clown who learned how to tie a decent knot in Scouts so many years ago.

*

I can't stop remembering that first time I saw you in seminary twenty-seven years ago. I had wandered through the ornate library searching for some great theologian willing to take on Aquinas' proofs of the existence of God, not because I didn't believe in God. I just wanted to recover the feminine nature of the God who I knew would always be with me.

Then you appeared, my rock, like Peter in the Bible, you told me. That's what you became. How could I have been so wrong? But paper covers rock. You used to say that. What had you papered over? *Mea maxima culpa*. How I misjudged you. You showed me around the feminists – Chittister, Fiorenza and Radford Ruether. I was touched, though years later I realized you had immersed yourself in the depths of their radical search for the voices of women so you could destroy their arguments and keep your orthodox soul afloat. It took me a long time to figure that out. I was too entranced by your inarguable charm, the flick of your wrist across your sleek locks, your (I thought) genuine attempt to engage my questioning heart. My faint heart. My stupid heart.

*

I don't talk about this in Group. Not to that soldier who lost his leg in Iraq. Nor to that statue, the queen of the Caribbean, stately in gold and purple – but stunningly silent. Derek says she lost her man to that government programme that sends Jamaicans home. Windrush Two. Some folks in my congregation call it a 'reverse boat people' effort that will 'cleanse' the nation, as if they've never heard a single sermon that I have preached for the past two decades. I despair. I feel sad for this woman.

I have seen the Caribbean queen around our village, the soldier too, though not often. The village is a quiet corner in the capital marked by a high street and narrow footpath that circles shops where locals meet and strangers nod as they dodge one another to avoid collisions. There's the vegetable shop, churches, the pub with the England-shirt skinheads outside flicking cigarette butts onto the roadway, a bookshop with paperbacks and magazines on display, and the unisex hair place, though I don't go there now. People are brutal when they get a whiff of a good old-fashioned sex scandal, a break-up in the manse, a younger woman.

Now it's worse.

I can't go anywhere. Takes me back to you. The humiliation. The pain. Your body. Hanging in my garden.

*

Derek is on the phone, reminding me about Group. He set up the Grief Group a while back. I went occasionally before. Enough said about that. Now he is leaning on me again.

I tell him we are not a group, that I am not grieving. Take

me off the list. He sighs softly into my mobile. There is a pause along the invisible line that connects our phones. I imagine him stroking that grey straggle, shaking his head from side to side, breaking into that sly smile. Then he whispers a solemn invocation. 'Now, Faith, we said we would just give this a chance.'

Did we?

Finally, I agree. I will go to Group.

'I don't think you will regret it, Faith.'

But I already do regret it.

*

This morning, I slip out the front door without glancing out the garden window. I sneak through the village with my head down, avoiding eye contact.

The joy of our village has always been bumping into neighbours, members of the congregation, Zac, the hairdresser. No more. I wander past shops where I used linger, look for sales, spring hats, new books, or scan the photos in the estate agents' windows, find out how much my tiny manse would sell for.

I keep moving, don't talk to anyone, stop at the pharmacy to pick up my prescription.

I am on my way to Group in Derek's old home near the heath. Only he knows why I first dragged myself to his comfortable living room to bear my soul. It wasn't just the separation from Peter three years ago.

There are four of us in a circle on comfortable old chairs, each cradling a coffee cup, tea mug or plastic water bottle. Derek speaks softly, nudges us to open up about our 'Godforsaken grief'. The queen of the Caribbean smiles at me, and I catch myself smiling back. Derek talks about what he calls 'the now well-recognized stages of grief' first identified in the 1960s. I remember studying them in seminary. Peter always said they were a liberal mythology concocted by a frustrated nun. I used to think he was wrong. I'm no longer sure. They feel too structured – 1, 2, 3 4, 5. There is no order to what is happening to me.

Derek wants us all to say a few words about how we are feeling. I am doing fine until he asks that. The queen of the Caribbean's name is Sophia. She is a retired nurse who came from Jamaica many years ago at the request of the NHS. She says, 'Me, I am having one of my better days, though I still miss my man, Charles, stuck back in our original home – Jamaica. We talk on the telephone but some days he is too sad or unwell. I know our government here will do the right thing and let him return.'

Derek looks my way and I just shake my head – not yet. He turns to the soldier, who slowly rolls up his trouser leg, unstraps his prosthesis, lays it down beside his chair. He begins talking about the war and losing his leg in a bloody battle. The skirmish still gives him nightmares.

'The only way I can sleep is by taking these pills the GP gave me,' Josh, the soldier, says, flipping open a Velcro pocket and producing the plastic bottle of pills. 'When I sleep that deeply I'm back in the war. There's a great explosion and a burning fire in my leg, or I should say, where my leg should be. I wake up, crying. And can't get back to sleep. This is my regime, day in, day out. I don't know how long I can carry on. My girlfriend split months ago. I miss her, but, frankly, I miss my leg, my life ... Sorry.'

He blows his nose on a tissue, stops talking. Looks toward Derek as if to say, 'Rescue me.'

I am about to respond but ...

Derek looks at his watch and says, 'I think that's all for today.'

I get up and leave.

*

I walk to the park and find a quiet bench overlooking the City, its skyscrapers and cranes making it appear like some kind of mechanical toy city in a child's bedroom. I can't bear to think of such a room. My tea is cool now, but I sip it intermittently. It's always this way. One of the few things that hasn't changed over the past three months. I sit for what seems a long time, wondering about the voice I hear in my sleep, and about tomorrow's appointment with my GP, about the uselessness of Group. I begin to feel the late evening breeze and decide to get up. As I do, Sophia suddenly appears and sits down beside me. I sit back down. The bench creaks on one side, then the other.

Sophia is a big woman, dressed in bright colours I would never get away with. She wears a scent I have noticed before, that reminds me of spring blossoms in my garden. For the first time, I see that she is beautiful. Up close, even more lovely. Her smile is warm, her breathing slow, calming. I have never said one word to her in all the times I have seen her in the village, or in Group. Why? I am not yet sure I want to talk to her. But here she is. Sophia reaches across the bench and touches my arm. I shiver.

'I've missed you, Faith. I just wanted to thank you for coming out to Group again,' she says, her Caribbean accent like music.

I can't help myself. I laugh.

'Yes, I've contributed so much,' I say.

Her smile is broad and generous. 'I too have said little. But I see we are sisters in grief. Wouldn't you say?'

'I don't know. Our situations are different. Your husband was sent back to Jamaica, right?'

'Yes, I miss him very much. Group reminds me, though, that I am not alone in this grief.'

I don't want to talk about grief.

I ask, 'Is he a nurse too?'

'He was a porter, an orderly, a cleaner.' She laughs. 'Anything that was needed. He wanted to keep working. To support our family, especially when I took time out from nursing to raise our children. He's a good man. I miss him. And he is now ill. The doctors say he may not have long to live.'

'Can you visit him?'

'My lawyer says, "Don't go or they will not let you come back".'

'That's horrible. And your children?'

'They are here, a boy and a girl, both married with children of their own. I am "Nana" to two girls and one boy. "Nana" – my favourite word.'

'That's lovely.'

'And you, Faith. Do you have children?'

'No.' I spit it out.

'Hmm.'

I start to say something more. Stop. Begin to shiver slightly. Wipe my eyes.

'When you are ready, you will say more, maybe.'

'Maybe,' I respond quietly. 'I'm not sure.'

'Next time, we should meet here afterwards again,' Sophia says, as she rises from the bench to the creak of the ancient boards. She hands me a card with her name and telephone number. 'Or call me if you want to talk.'

I look up at her.

She touches me on the shoulder, gently. And, for the first time in months, I hear myself say, 'I'd like that.'

I sit a while on my own in silence.

Then I hear that voice again.

Now I fly with the angels
Learning love can mean forgive.
Floating above life's riddles
Praying the pain, you outlive.

Anger

I finally go to see my GP. It's quiet in the waiting room as a fox rambles through the back garden without a worry, even at midday. There's a beep. My name comes up on the digital screen above the windows. Room 15. I climb the stairs.

My GP, who has been to the house once and telephoned several times over the past weeks, lifts a sheet of paper from the top of a small pile of documents on her desk and hands it to me. She looks weary, sweeping her long brown hair out of her dark eyes – and it makes me worry. I thank her for coming to see me, for phoning, for answering my call. She waves her hand.

And yet, when she speaks, I become more worried.

'We'll need more tests, but the initial diagnosis looks problematic. It most likely explains the headaches, but we're not sure yet whether we should operate or just monitor the situation. The consultant will help you understand what the future holds.'

A few minutes later, I wander out of her office in a daze, like I am sleepwalking.

'Looks problematic,' I whisper to myself, all the way home.

*

A week later, I slip out of the house without looking out the garden window. I know you are there, hanging there, killing my love for the garden, for life itself.

I go to Group again. There are several new members, alongside me, Josh and Sophia. Derek smiles in my direction, begins talking about the nun's stages of grief again, about anger that those left behind after a death or other loss might suffer. I fight the urge to get up and leave.

Josh says some days he wants to get a gun from his old barracks and go shoot someone, take out a whole shopping mall like they do in America. He begins weeping and again takes off his prosthesis.

Sometimes I wonder how many people he killed in Iraq, soldiers, civilians, collateral damage, all for the good cause. I know this is harsh. He has been through Hell twice, in Iraq and back in the United Kingdom. Depressed, he can't work. Many months, he finds himself in arrears and is worried about paying his rent.

'Would anyone like to respond to Josh's intervention?' Derek asks.

Silence.

Derek then breaks the silence. He's been reading my mind.

'This remains a safe place for each and every one of you to speak of your losses. We do not judge. So, thank you, Josh. The grieving process will be different for each of us. When you are ready, we will listen to you as well. This is a safe place.'

He looks in my direction, checks his watch. We are finished.

I look across the circle at Sophia. I see a slight nod of her head in my direction. We will talk later.

Sophia has brought tea and lemon cakes from her church social to our weary bench in the park. She was speaking to Josh, she says, explaining why she is later than we had agreed. Away from Group, Sophia seems happier. I don't think I ever smile any more. Still, the sun is beginning to peek through the clouds that have made the morning even more gloomy for me.

'Josh's story is very sad,' Sophia says. 'My son was in the army for a while but left before signing up permanently. We were both very relieved. That could have been him losing a leg in some Godforsaken battle, in some horrible part of the world.'

'What's your son's name?' I feel like I am shifting into counselling mode, seminary training I haven't used in many weeks. Training I thought I had lost since that morning – *that* morning.

'Martin, after Martin Luther King Jr.' She says this proudly, as if she knew the American civil rights leader personally. She lifts her head towards the sky.

We are quiet, sipping our tea, enjoying the lemon cake. Across the heath, a small unruly-looking group of youngsters and an old man with a cane are singing and whooping in some kind of religious or political rally.

'What's happening there?' I wonder.

'I know that old man,' Sophia says. 'From my church. We're Baptists. He used to be a great preacher, a lay preacher. Gone astray, perhaps, but still a good man, I think.'

'Wonder what it's all about?'

'I will look in on them later,' Sophia says. 'How are you doing, Faith? After today? After our last conversation? After everything you have been through?'

Everything. That word makes me grip my cup of tea too

tightly. I spill some on the front of my green raincoat.

'Oh dear. These things happen,' Sophia says, immediately producing a tissue to help wipe up. How does she always seem to have the right thing at the right time? Tea, cake, tissues.

'Thank you. You're good in a crisis.'

'I was a nurse,' she says. 'A good nurse.'

'Is there any other kind?' I ask.

'Oh, yes,' she laughs.

We sip our tea, finish off the lemon cake.

'You have seen a lot of death, a lot of deaths, as a nurse, I mean,' I whisper.

'Naturally.'

'There's nothing natural about suicide,' I say, surprising myself, but not Sophia.

'I don't know. Maybe you are right. Maybe not. Many people take it upon themselves to decide when to die. I don't know if that is natural or unnatural. I try not to judge.'

'Is that because you are a Baptist or a nurse?' An honest question.

Sophia laughs. 'God knows. Maybe a bit of both. "Judge not" – I find that freeing somehow.'

'You know about my husband – ex-husband, I should say – killing himself in my back garden, Sophia?' I say this quietly.

I am not sure she hears me as a minute passes before she responds.

'Yes. I am so sorry, Faith.'

Sophia squeezes my hand. I feel the warmth of her, and the cool gold of her wedding band.

'Thank you.'

We are silent for a long time. Police cars and an ambulance arrive across the heath where the old man and the youngsters have been rallying.

Sophia looks over, shakes her head. 'Oh dear.'

'Do you want to go see what is happening?' I ask her.

'There is nothing I can do there, I don't think. I want to sit with you a little longer. I think I should stay with you.'

'Thank you.'

After a while, Sophia asks: 'Did you still love him?'

What?

But I can't say it out loud. I choose my words carefully.

'Our love died a long time before he died.'

The words sound harsh even to me.

'Hmm.'

'You don't believe me?'

'I believe you think so, but you'd been intimate with that man a long time; loved him, lost him, now can't talk about him, but can't stop thinking about him. Love like that changes but I am not sure it dies.'

'You're starting to sound like Derek.'

I feel my face flush.

'Sorry,' I say.

'No need. I understand,' Sophia responds.

Sophia makes like she is getting ready to leave, reaches for her big olive-coloured handbag.

'I hear him. I hear his voice. I think he is telling me things. But it's all riddles. I wonder if I'm going mad. Do you think I'm crazy?' I ask Sophia.

'You're grieving, Faith.'

'There you go, sounding like Derek again. You ought to set up a practice.'

Sophia laughs quietly.

'Derek's not so bad, Faith. He's just maybe a bit too "textbook" sometimes.'

'A bit too male,' I retort, regretting it immediately.

Sophia ignores the remark.

'The voice?' Sophia continues, 'Do you answer back?'

'I don't have to. I think he knows my every thought.'

We leave it there.

Sophia heads back to the village.

I sit.

I hear the voice again.

Here we see no boundaries
Between the loved and the lost,
Among the dead and living
Angels and mortals are tossed.

*

Tom has finally managed to locate Peter's estranged sister, Lizzie, in Australia. Today, after this long delay, the funeral is being held in my church. The pews are polished. The scent turns my stomach. Lizzie arrives, looking fit and in anything but mournful mood. She hugs me, says, 'G'day' and plants herself beside me in the front row of the sparsely populated nave. A few of the elderly parishioners from Peter's church and some from mine trudge in silently and sit in the rows behind us. Derek and Josh enter at the last minute and I turn to watch them sit down glumly. We are all on one side of the church, helping us feel like a real mourning congregation.

Tom is taking the service. He is at his best. The altar servers are wearing red soutanes and white surplices. The incense brings tears to my eyes. Tom preaches about God's forgiveness. He is eloquent, biblical, warm, understanding. I can't bear it. I go to get up and leave in the midst of Tom's homily. Lizzie discreetly grabs my arm, pulling me back.

'Stay, sis.'

Tom pronounces those familiar words from Ecclesiastes, 'All go to one place; all are from the dust; and all turn to dust again.'

'*I'm* not ready for that place,' I whisper to myself.

Lizzie disappears right after the service, with a hug and a squeeze of my hand. Tom says he will meet up with her before she flies home, to offer any support he can. There is no burial. Lizzie plans to take Peter's ashes to Australia and toss them into the wind at her beachfront cottage.

I try to thank Tom for the service, but he waves me away, disappears out the side door of the church, where his partner Francis is probably waiting in their Union Jack Mini. They are off on a long-postponed holiday in Spain. I wonder how I will cope without him as I return to ministering to my flock.

A few congregants stay afterwards for tepid tea, soup and egg sandwiches, courtesy of our dwindling ladies group. I go to thank them, and they greet me with long hugs, whispered words I can't quite take in. I have been on sick leave since Peter's death. Tom has been running things. Somehow, they have not forgotten me.

Then I hear that voice once more.

> *Is this the end of living?*
> *Or just one more beginning?*
> *Is the Earth renewed again?*
> *Is Heaven imbued again?*

Bargaining

I hear those words echo in my soul as I wander the streets of the village for the first time in many weeks after the funeral. I don't know why I am feeling so brave. The sun is shining, some familiar faces nod in my direction on the crowded footpath – Zac, the hairdresser; the harassed young man who owns the bookshop placing a table of classic paperbacks outside; one of the new members of Group, though he looks down as I pass.

I think about the voice and I want to respond to it: you never waxed poetic. Your words were harsh, without rhythm.

I remember one conversation we had when you returned to the village one time.

We were sitting outside the café, watching the shoppers strip down as the rain stopped and the sun came out. They were desperate for the warmth the sun brought. We were gloomy.

You gave a grand speech about the state of our relationship as prams rolled by and the mums and dads checked their phones.

'You never could accept the fact that even though I went through seminary, got ordained and served as a priest all those years, I could then change directions, find my own way.'

'Wait a minute, you left with that near-adolescent

Sunday-school teacher. Left me, left your congregation.'

'I was leaking pain like a slit wrist leaks blood. What I received, from you, from your church, and my church, was judgement. "Judge not" is what they preach. Actions speak louder than words. Your righteousness is rich. "Love your neighbour," not just when he plays the straight-and-narrow game of marriage and family but when he is compelled to satisfy his search for freedom. That's when the love evaporates.'

Then you got up and left me alone with my cold coffee and my tears.

At least that's how I remember it.

*

A five-year-old child has gone missing in the village. In our little village! His name is Bogdan and he is the son of one of the Romanian women who sell The Big Issue at the station. I have seen him with his mother over the past year, a quiet child wearing a red football shirt and kicking a ball against the outside wall of the station. Just *five*.

Today, everyone on the village footpaths shakes their heads in disbelief. 'Horrible,' I hear the butcher whisper as he unfurls the awning. I nod in agreement. People huddle in twos or threes in quiet conversations on the high street, covering their mouths like footballers on television who don't want viewers to know the colour of their banter. I keep my head down. My aching head.

Sophia's Baptist church ladies are handing out tea, coffee and cheese sandwiches to the police and the volunteers scouring the heath and the park that border our village. Sophia sent me a message first thing this morning, wondering if our women could help. I'm on my way to her church; two or three others from my women's group will meet me there.

There are tables outside in the sunshine and several women are serving tea and coffee to the volunteers. Inside, I head to the kitchen and help Sophia, who is washing up.

'Terrible,' she says, though she looks like she is exactly where she wants to be. Helping out. 'Thanks for coming, Faith. Your ladies are lovely.'

'They are,' I agree.

'How are you doing?' she asks.

'I thought I was getting stronger. But this ... I don't know.'

'We have a prayer group in the chapel, in there.' She points her soapy finger up a half-flight of stairs. 'We can go there when we finish this lot if you want. Say a few prayers for that boy.'

'I don't know.'

'I've been here for nearly forty years and I've never heard of a child going missing like this.'

'Me neither.' I spit this out.

I see from her raised eyebrow she finds my response too quick, so change the subject. 'I hear your friend died that day on the heath. I am so sorry, Sophia. What happened?'

'They said it was a heart attack, but the police used a Taser on him. I don't know what to think.'

'A Taser?'

Sophia sighs heavily. 'It is very sad. The funeral was here, the same day as your Peter's, otherwise you know I would have been there, Faith.'

'I understand.'

We stack the cleaned and dried dishes and take them to the ladies outside of the church who are on a break, sitting quietly at the tables and taking in the sunshine. We head back inside. Sophia takes me by the arm to guide me up the steps to the chapel and we sit quietly in the back row on ornate benches that remind me of the ones in Peter's church. It's quiet. All I can hear is Sophia's breathing. Her eyes are shut, and she is praying, or taking a moment's respite. She does look weary.

I can't pray. I haven't been able to pray for many weeks.. Either God is not there, or I can't reach her. I just think of the missing boy, Bogdan, five years old. *Five.* I can't bear it.

After a while, we return to the kitchen. A group of searchers arrives, and we make cheese and tomato sandwiches and big pots of tea. Sophia sings under her breath, 'Jesus loves me, this I know. For the Bible tells me so ...'

I can't bring myself to join in this simple but beautiful hymn, one I have always loved.

Then I hear the voice yet again.

> *When human hearts are broken*
> *And the godless are to blame*
> *It's time to change the music*
> *And to wash away the shame.*

*

Today is my first Sunday service after three months of relying on Tom and several members of the congregation who can put together a service that looks, sounds and feels like an Anglican service. That sounds unkind. It probably is. One of my many sins of late. God, forgive me.

The lectionary calls for me to preach on Jesus telling his disciples that, much as they might have thought he would bring peace to their families and tranquillity to their communities, he will actually bring division. It's in Luke. It's not one of my favourite passages.

Peter used to say, 'Tell them it's one of those passages Jesus didn't really mean,' or, 'Suggest he was just misquoted.' That always sounded too easy a way out for me. However, I have never known quite how to handle it. Today it seems near impossible.

These days, you go online and find all varieties of explanations, from the ultra-conservative to Peter's kind of waffling he-didn't-really-mean-it sort of explanations. God, how he had moved from orthodoxy. A Roman Catholic commentator suggested that it is all about short-term pain for long-term gain. None of this online theology rings true to me and so today, after Luke is read by a young girl from Ghana and a gentle hymn sung slightly out of tune by our ageing soloist, I go out beyond our sculpted wooden pulpit and sit down among the twenty worshippers, mostly women my age and older, and just talk to them.

'The truth is, I don't really know what Jesus was saying in the passage we are asked to reflect on today. I trust that we should love our families, but I know sometimes it is very hard to do. People sometimes do horrible things to one another. And sometimes it must be very hard to love us, too. We too have done some pretty rotten things. Perhaps that's all I can say today.'

I stand up and turn away from the congregation to return to the front of the church, catch myself, turn around and say, 'Sorry... I mean, Amen.'

We sing another hymn and then one of the elders enters the pulpit to make the weekly announcements. It seems the amalgamation talks with St. Mary's are moving rapidly towards a conclusion. I missed that. Missed so very much.

Then I say, 'Go in peace to love one another.'

I can barely get the words out, but I make it through. Thank God.

I wander across the green lawns to my tiny home, once my refuge, now the place where you hang, with your secrets exposed, and mine too. And I hear the voice again, stark, stirring.

> *Tragedy brings us closer*
> *To the night that killed the love*
> *A boy's lost, a body found*
> *We search the skies for the dove.*
>
> *

The next morning Sophia phones, waking me from a deep and disturbing sleep. The police have found a body. The search for Bogdan is off. And there is something else in her voice, normally so strong – a cracking, breaking. I first thought it was the phone line, but no. She is crying. What else has gone wrong?

'Faith, I need to talk to you – today, now.'

It's my day off but I don't hesitate. 'Come here, right away, Sophia. I'll put the kettle on.'

I hang up and then brush my frazzled hair, put on an old pair of jeans and a T-shirt, wash my face and hands, go downstairs. Will she see you hanging in my back garden? I have not told her about this.

We will sit at the kitchen table. You will be out of sight. Out of mind? I hope so.

The doorbell rings. Sophia brings digestives, her favourite biscuits. Maybe she is okay. But no, I see her puffy eyes and damp cheeks. She has been crying.

'I'm so sorry about Bogdan,' I say, praying (yes praying) that there is nothing more to be sorry about.

'That family will be devastated,' Sophia says. 'They have already decided to go back to Romania, for the funeral, and then stay. They have not been happy here for a long time. People are not buying the magazine anymore and some even stop to yell, "Go home, where you belong".'

'God, that's horrible,' I say.

Then I add without thinking, 'We should have saved that boy.'

My God.

Sophia looks up from her tea, stares straight at me for a second or two without breathing a word.

What have I said?

'Do the police say what happened to the boy?' I ask quickly.

'Not yet,' Sophia's voice is weak. 'But I fear the worst. This was not an accident. This has been a horrible night.'

'Yes, it has,' I say, not fully understanding, perhaps not wanting to.

The tea is too hot and we both put our mugs down on the kitchen table for a few moments, sit in silence. Sophia's eyes are puffy. She has not slept. She wants to say something more, but she hesitates. I wait a while, blow softly on my milky tea, take another sip.

Finally, she speaks.

'My dear husband, Charles, has died in Jamaica. May he rest in peace. This is truly my saddest day. Faith, my friend, I must go to the funeral. I will leave soon, very soon. They will not let me back into this country because of this Windrush business.'

Sophia covers his face with her hands

'It is so cruel,' I whisper.

We both break down in tears. I hold her in my arms a long time. Soon we move to the front door. She has so much to do but we agree to speak later in the week. I need to talk to her. She knows this.

Depression

Bogdan is dead. Sophia is leaving. My congregation is disintegrating. You are still hanging in my garden.

I want out of the house, so I take a long walk through the village, gloomy under dark clouds with no one looking up from their shopping or cups of coffee. The butcher grunts into his bin as he carries it round the back of his shop. The bookshop is closed. I head for the park, look for the bench where Sophia and I have talked, but it is occupied by a homeless man lying under an old army coat. I hear him snoring as I get close, so I know he is alive. Him, at least. The rain starts up and I walk more quickly to the old statue that overlooks the City, but turn quickly, pull up my hood and head back home.

I pause and look at my old church. It's beautiful, shrouded in the evening rain. The wooden cross above the doorway is daunting, creating a dark shadow, even in the cloudburst. I think about going inside to say a prayer for Bogdan, and one for Sophia, maybe even one for myself. Instead I cross the overgrown lawn and go home. I ignore the back garden and head upstairs. I shut the bedroom door behind me. I need four walls closed around me. I need to rest. I need to sleep. I need to dream. I close my eyes.

I hear the voice again.

> *I have met the little one*
> *Embraced him with weary arms.*
> *He's no longer just a boy*
> *But an angel now unharmed.*

*

Another day. Don't look out that window. Don't think about you. Get out of the house. Stay among the living.

Group is meeting at Derek's home. Derek has only invited Josh, Sophia and me. This is Sophia's farewell. Josh limps in a few minutes after the rest of us, carrying a single red rose for Sophia. She takes a deep breath, then rises to accept the flower from him, and they share a long, warm hug. I wonder if she has been meeting with Josh as well. I shouldn't be surprised. Derek looks over his specs at me, smiling.

Derek begins, 'Today we say goodbye to our dear Sophia. We are so sorry for your loss, for the death of Charles in Jamaica. We know you must return there for his funeral. But we are grieving over the loss of you from our Group, our village, our community.'

I may not make it through this.

We each talk about how much we have learned over the past few months from Sophia, how much we will miss her, how much we love her. I am last to speak and take my time getting started.

'I have been – I don't want to use that G-word – *missing* you already, from the moment I heard about Charles dying. I am so sorry for your loss. Your husband sounds like a good man. You love him, have loved him all this time and even while he returned to Jamaica. I am so sorry to see you go. You have touched me and helped me. I will always call you' – I wipe my eyes – 'my dearest friend.'

I look at Derek and his nodding tells me he has been wise to my long talks with Sophia. That maybe they were even part of his plan.

Tears run down my cheek. I can't look at anyone.

Sophia responds quietly. 'Thank you all. We have been on this road together. Derek has put the petrol in our little black cab. We all have taken turns driving.'

I know this is not true. I have been too slow to reach out. Sadness over this truth wells up in me and I need to be on my own. I get up to go to the toilet, maybe to escape through Derek's back door.

Sophia's voice stops me. 'Faith wants to tell us what first brought her to Group.'

'I'm sorry, I do not.'

Derek clears his throat, says, 'I think maybe …'

Sophia speaks over him, gently but firmly. 'My dear, Faith. Today is my last day with you, all of you. Tell us why you have come here so many months ago. I think we know now it was not just your husband leaving nearly four years ago. We mourn with you over his recent suicide. You have told me that he speaks to you even now. Is it possible that he is trying to talk to you, *grieve* with you about what brought you here?'

I cannot speak. I cannot breathe. I cannot stop crying.

The room is silent. The traffic outside has died down. Church bells ring on the heath but the wind muffles the tolling, as if making way for my response. I grip the arms of my chair.

I look up and Josh – that brute of a soldier – is weeping. Derek stares at his sandals. Sophia peers straight at me.

A long silence.

Then I whisper, 'He was just five days old.'

> *Now is the time to confess*
> *The secrets of my lost soul.*
> *Five days' love was blessing*
> *But his last breath left us cold.*
>
> *

Cot death. Two simple words. No explanation. No reasons. No answers. No medical diagnosis. No scientific theories. No theological rationalization. Nothing. Just two words. That's all they told me. Doctors. Psychiatrists. Counsellors. Pastors. Cot death. The only answer I could give when the inevitable question was asked. Cot death. For days, weeks, months, the words came to me in the morning and stayed in my head all day. Preparing sermons on the love of God. Cot death. Eating dinner. Cot death. Doing the washing up. Cot death. Watching the television news. Cot death. Elders' meeting. Cot death. Going to bed. Cot death. Waking up. Cot death.

Our love could not save him. Nothing could. A part of me died in that cot with our son. A part of *us* died in that cot with our son. Something also grew out of that death, a cancer that flourished in me, and in you, killed our love, killed our affection, killed our marriage.

I carried Waldo in my heart every day. There was no room for Peter. He carried Waldo in his heart every day. There was no room for me. They say the heart expands to embrace all kinds of crises. Somehow, we could not make it happen.

Cot death.

*

I keep my bargain with myself and head out the front door without looking at your now ragged corpse in my scruffy back garden. I walk through the village wearing my summer hat and sunglasses. I pretend no one knows me and that I am a stranger in my own village. We are suffering through another heatwave and so I can avoid engaging with my neighbours today. I have barely been out of doors since Sophia left.

Because it is holiday time, joint services are being held at Peter's old church, with Tom leading the few souls unable to escape to the seaside, giving those attending the opportunity to enjoy his lovely chanting Taizé rite. I love the quiet rhythm of the music and Tom's voice gives the accompanying meditations a depth I can never match. His services rarely nudge the congregation to engage in the world, certainly not the political world, but he reaches people in ways I never will.

The bench where Sophia and I talked a month or so ago is empty. I sit down and listen to its familiar creaking. I can sense Sophia presence beside me, and I begin to talk to her. No one is around but I don't really care if they come. This all needs saying.

'Seminary studies and the early days of our marriage were like swimming in cool clear waters that were always refreshed. We laughed so much, debated social gospel, liberation theology, justification by faith alone, Jesus as Lord, Jesus as son of God; we made love so often we both fell away laughing at how outrageously good it was and how drenched we were with sweat and bodily fluids; we married quietly in the school chapel with a few good friends from seminary. It all felt so natural, so easy, so perfect. After ordination, we served as curates in two rural parishes near the seminary. Of course, babies would come.

'It wasn't a difficult pregnancy, really. No different from any of my friends. Yes, I was sick many mornings, got so big I could barely move at the end and for a while Peter had to help out in my parish as well as his. Though he was always too conservative for my lot. The birth was hard but 'normal' – that's the word the midwife used.

'We brought him home wrapped in a blue blanket. He was pink, and to our eyes, perfect. We cried as we laid him in the cot that night. Cried for joy. Walter. Our joy. We called him Walter – after my father – but from the first moment he set him down in the cot, Peter dubbed him 'Waldo'. He'd been reading Ralph Waldo Emerson. Somehow, it fit.

The park is still deserted, and I stand to shake off the crumbs from the fruit scone I have been nibbling as I speak to the absent Sophia. I sit back down, feel the breeze, finally some respite from the heat. I imagine Sophia shifting on the bench beside me, reaching her pudgy hand towards me, encouraging me to continue.

'We buried him in an unmarked grave in the cemetery of the country church where I was curate. Only Peter and I know where Waldo lies. There was no funeral, neither of us could face that. The first of many mistakes. For a long time, Peter slept on a mattress in Waldo's room. I didn't discourage this. A mistake. I lay alone in our bed without sleep or his comfort.

'We needed to get away from the country churches, so we took up parishes around the corner from one another in this village, thanks to a benevolent bishop Peter knew. We threw ourselves into our ministries. He took his congregation on a spiritual retreat. He said it gave them new vision. He was never the same. I never bothered to find out who he had become.

'Gloria was her name. A Sunday-school teacher. At first there were suggestions she was underage. That's what the ladies in my congregation told me. She was of age. Barely. Not that it lasted. There was no hope after that. Even though we tried to get back together. He came weeping in the front door. I took him in, but I had nothing to offer. I have to admit, I couldn't really forgive him. Not just Gloria. But for how he mocked my continuing faith while he had sought the truth in a mindless search for pleasure. How he abandoned me, his congregation, his faith. At one point, he begged me to take him back. I took him into our bed. We were animals for an hour. Not lovers. Not like we once were. We knew it wouldn't last. It didn't last. There were too many of us in the bed. He and I; Gloria; Waldo.

'He wandered around the country after that. Wrote a book on something he called Christian Atheism. Had numerous young lovers. I tried not to care.

'There, I said it. That's me done.

'Thanks, Sophia.'

No response. Just the breeze shaking the trees.

I head home, stripping off my hat and sunglasses as I go, feeling a bit of life in my weary legs. God knows why.

Mistakes and misdemeanours
Memories go marching on.
Make the most of the moment
Or all the love will be gone.

Acceptance

It's foggy outside though I see you hanging there, now more like a dream than a reality. I suddenly worry you are not comfortable with that rope burning your neck. Then I realize what a ridiculous thought this is. I turn away, leave the house and cross to my tiny office in the church. I haven't been here in weeks and it is a mess of unopened post, cobwebs, dust. I dig in.

Tom arrives unexpectedly. It's his day off. He looks slightly dishevelled. Hair mussy like the Prime Minister's, collarless and in jeans. I make a place for him by moving a heap of post off the second chair in my study and he sits, leaning in towards me but looking at the crucifix above the desk behind me.

'You alright, Tom?' I ask.

'Good, good,' he says quickly, though we both know better.

'Do you want to go over the preaching schedule? Is it the amalgamation talks?'

The conversations have been going well and it appears that within the next six months, St, Margaret's will be amalgamating with Peter's flock, St. Mary's.

Tom interrupts my thoughts.

'It seems they want me for the vacancy, for the amalgamation,' Tom says

I laugh out loud. Of course. I should have seen this coming. I haven't paid enough attention to that side of the parish life recently – any side. The laughter feels good and I let out another great roar. The first time in ... years.

'Faith, I'm not sure my call to ministry is that funny.'

'Dear Tom, I know that your ministry is truly wonderful. You saved my life so many times in the past few months. You and Sophia, Derek, Josh, and the ladies here. I'm laughing because this makes so much sense. I thought *I* had a decision to make. But you are the best candidate. Oh, Tom, you have my blessing – if you want it.'

I have to stop him from kissing me a hundred times on each cheek, then I send him on his way. Halfway out the door, he phones Francis to tell him the good news. Somehow, I feel better than I have for months.

I sit in my study for a long time, ignore the mess of paper and dust around me, and think, pray.

'Dear God, what next?'

I'm due an extended leave and, when the amalgamation is complete, I will take it. I need to read, walk, pray, remember, forget. I will visit Sophia in Jamaica, sit by the sea with her in the tiny fishing village. It will be wonderful just to see her, talk to her. Her emails have been few and succinct, but she says I would be welcome to visit her village.

'It is a simple life,' she cautions. 'It's not a thriving village like you have there.'

I can see her smile as she taps this into her computer.

First, there is another visit I must make, a longer journey. I rummage through the piles of paper and find the phone number Tom unearthed for me months ago. I pick up the phone and call Lizzie in Australia, forgetting the time difference. No matter: she picks up on the first ring.

'Sis,' she says, 'Are you coming to visit me in Oz?'

'Yes, I am.'

'Wonderful. The ashes are waiting for you to come help me scatter them,' Lizzie says.

> There are no walls that divide
> Only a circle of time.
> Life begins on God's good Earth
> Continues in states divine.
>
> *

This morning you are but a ghost hanging in my back garden. I can still make out your cocked head, your bloated body. I begin to open the glass doors to approach but then turn away.

It is my last Sunday at church. Tom has organized a farewell service that he will lead. The bishop will read scripture and I will preach. There will be incense, lots of incense, traditional hymns, though Tom has included my modern favourite, 'I, the Lord of Sea and Sky'. Sea and sky. Tom knows Australia and Jamaica beckon. His perfectly attired partner, Francis, sits in the front row staring directly at the portly bishop, who pays him no heed. I am across the aisle. Derek and Josh sit with me. There are sixty people in the church Tom encouraged many from the other congregation to attend.

The bishop makes his way slowly to the pulpit, puts on his spectacles and opens the big red Bible at the Gospel of Saint Luke, reading the few lines I requested: 'You shall love the Lord your God with all your heart, and with all your soul, and with all your strength, and with all your mind; and your neighbour as yourself.'

Now it is my turn to speak.

I have notes in front of me, but I can barely see them through the mist of my emotion. I am leaving this congregation after more than two decades. I am buying the house from the diocese as part of the amalgamation, though I have pledged to stay away from church services.

Of course, I will keep the garden as well. I have married and buried too many to count in this place where God is supposed to be present. Many times, I have felt her presence – in the praying, the singing, the weeping, the laughter. Lately, I have not found her, though today I wonder if I have not looked in the right places.

'Thank you,' I say finally. 'Thank you for showing me how both parts of that calling are possible. I have seen you love God in so many ways, your prayers, your Bible study, your singing of all the old hymns, and a few new ones on occasion.'

Some quiet laughter echoes throughout the old church

'Do you remember how easy love once was?'

A few eyebrows arch upwards, including Tom's. He is seated next to Francis for my sermon. I smile at him. He'll be okay, this young priest.

'Love isn't always easy,' I continue. 'In fact, sometimes it dies. Or we let it die. Are we called to love only in the good times? Only the good people? If that were the case, we wouldn't really need Jesus as our guide, would we? So, how do we love those who hurt us? Abandon us? Cheat on us?

'And,' I pause, then add, 'How do they love us when we have failed them?

'I must confess that not only have I been failed in love, but I have failed in love.

'So, I only have these questions this morning. No answers. Sorry.

'I am going away now, on leave, to try and find out more about this, this God who loves me, who is always with me, and whose love I ought to be able to receive and pass on.

'I wish you well in your ministry here with Tom. Love him as you have loved me. Your love will be more than enough. Amen.'

I sit back down in my front seat and feel a weight lifted off my bent shoulders, as if I had been that maple tree holding that dead body. I think of the great debates about the nature of God in seminary that Peter and I loved so much. About the early days of our marriage. The romance. The bodily love. And, I think, too, of sweet Waldo, a treasure lost before we got to know him. How we barely had time to love him.

I feel the sweaty palm of that brute soldier, Josh, holding my hand. He whispers, 'Well said, Faith.'

Derek hands me a tissue, motioning towards my wet cheeks. 'Thank you,' I say.

Tom is back up front, announcing, 'Our final hymn is "I, the Lord of Sea and Sky".' The congregation stands and sings with unusual gusto, perhaps to say 'Goodbye' or 'Thank you,' or 'Thank God, she's gone.' I sing along. The bishop leaves before the hymn ends. He nods gracefully in my direction and squeezes through the narrow side door

At the end of the hymn, the ladies group presents me with a bouquet of roses from the village flower shop, and a cheque to help me make my way through the skies to the sea-surrounded islands.

I inhale the rich violet bouquet. I feel like I am halfway across the world already, flying under my own wings.

> *There are no perfect lovers*
> *They'll more likely make you fret,*
> *Yet even when you've lost them*
> *You'll never want to forget.*
>
> *

Lizzie casually pulls down the black metallic canister from atop her bookshelf, empties half the ashes into a smaller plastic container and hands the larger one to me. I place my share in my rucksack, put it in the guest room of her cottage on Kangaroo Island where I am lodged this week, then wander down to the crashing sea with Lizzie.

'Once upon a time Peter would have wanted us to utter some biblical wisdom at this moment,' Lizzie says over the sound of the crashing waves. 'However, from what I can gather, that's not where he was at in his last days.'

'I think you're probably right.'

'I think he'd given up on your God.'

'Maybe, but I wonder if he just wanted a rethink. He started off all very "old man in the sky righteous bearded God" in seminary, and when that didn't seem to work with the congregation, went from "invisible God" to "no God" to finding God in the arms of ...'

I stop myself. Maybe she didn't hear me, with the wind and the waves.

I suddenly remember the day we brought Waldo home from the hospital, wrapped in the blue blanket my Mum brought to the hospital. Such a beautiful sight. But I couldn't keep my eyes off Peter, flushed scarlet with joy as we got into the cab, giggling as he kissed Waldo's fuzzy little head. He couldn't stop talking, thinking ahead, questioning. His natural curiosity bubbling over.

'Such a miracle, this boy. Isn't he?'

'He is.'

We were both laughing and crying at the same time.

'I just want him to have everything he desires: love, family, books. I want him to have faith too, but to be a questioning kind of child.'

'Like his father.'

'Yes, why not? I think that's what gives me hope. The fact that we can carry on enjoying this life but asking big questions.'

'Well, he's just two days old. Let's not get ahead of ourselves. I've barely got him to latch on to my fat breasts.'

'Oh, he will. He'll be stuck to you for a long, long time.'

We laughed.

'That's a picture for the family album.'

We laughed again.

Yet, now I'm thinking that's a picture I would have cherished.

Strange how I had forgotten that conversation.

Lizzie's laugh brings me back to the present. She never seems to judge Peter, or me. Otherwise, I wouldn't have received this welcome to her cottage, a mile down the sandy shore from her partner, Agnes. Such a warm couple – two statuesque grey-haired beauties, perhaps kept together by living (slightly) apart. I start to ponder a sermon on boundaries in love, then remember I'm on leave.

I wish I hadn't said even as much as I had uttered just now with Lizzie. I should have talked about Waldo, the way we let our love die, the maple tree, my own part in it all. I should have mentioned that I actually admired how Peter had never shut down his inquiring – about who God was, whether God was, what life was all about.

Lizzie opens up the plastic container and charges towards the rolling waves, and there is a sudden, short and shocking streak of dust across the horizon, dancing before our eyes, then gone, scattered on to the beach, into the salty water and even on to our damp, ageing bodies.

'Farewell, brother,' Lizzie says. 'We'll see you soon enough,' she adds, a glitter in her eyes that might be tears.

'Amen,' I shout into the wind, turning my head away from Lizzie's view. 'Godspeed, Peter. Maybe see you sometime, somewhere,' I add.

> *I hear the gentle music*
> *All the songs of sea and sky*
> *Singing of our destiny*
> *A chorus before we die.*

*

I'm late this morning so don't look out at the back garden. I arrived home late last night, and the house is a mess and I imagine the garden is too. I don't let myself imagine anything more. I stop at the village bakery for their healthiest unhealthy breakfast, a blueberry muffin and black tea, carry them along past the bookshop – open again but with a man in a sharp suit behind the counter. I wonder where the worried young man who used to own the shop has gone. I pass the butcher who is outside unrolling his awning, as it looks like rain. Zac, the hairdresser, is reading a magazine, but looks up and waves. He points at my frazzled locks in mock shock. I think.

At my GP I wait until my name appears on the digital sign above the window. I'm the only one in the waiting room. I glance through magazines featuring colourful photos of healthy older people walking hand-in-hand along endless sandy beaches. Soon there is a beep from the digital sign, and I am summoned again to Room 15.

My GP is smiling, slightly.

'Faith, the consultant says you will not need surgery, not yet anyway. Maybe not at all. I think we can nip this in the bud – if you take care of yourself and check back with me in a few months' time.'

'I do have something I need to do, one more journey, then I'll be ready for the medical side of my recovery,' I say after my GP has provided me with NHS sheets, charts and graphs.

'Of course,' she says. 'It's all in this report. However, I want to see you back here in three months.'

I get on the phone as soon as I am back home and call Sophia. There is no answer, and her usual recording is garbled. I can't leave a message.

Never mind, there's something else I need to do. I grab my rucksack from the hall cupboard, put on my gardening duds, my gloves and hat, and head out to the back garden.

'God!'

You're not here, not hanging in my maple tree. No rope. No body, No cocked head. No bloated corpse. No stench.

I crash to the ground, landing on my knees. Thank God. I know I am being selfish but – thank God. You are gone.

I speak to you directly, aloud for once. 'I'm so sorry for the pain that brought you here. I share it. But I wanted – needed –

you gone from here. Or here, in a different way. There's been time enough for this grieving, this sadness.'

After a long silence where the wind is a mere whisper and for once there are no police sirens or ambulances, I whisper a prayer.

'Rest in peace.'

I get up off my knees, wipe the tears from my eyes. Tears for you. Finally.

I spend several hours cutting, pruning, weeding, clipping, raking, watering the garden. Then I cut the small patch of grass between the trees and add mulch and mix it in. I wrap a mile of electrician's tape around the plastic pipes that make up my ailing irrigation system, hoping that will put off the foxes. I turn it on, and it seems to be working, the rich soil gaining a darker, deeper hue. It won't be long before the worms are back digging away and the bees busy in my forsythias. Already, the back garden is coming to life again.

I sit and sip a cup of tea in a kind of altered state. I have my garden back. Well, to share with the blessed foxes.

I go and get the metal canister from my rucksack and take a handful of Peter's ashes to the maple tree. I spread the ashes around the trunk, patting them down into the soil, firmly but gently.

'Earth to earth.'

Then I go to the gnarled old dogwood. It is a scrubby little tree I have grown to love, particularly in those six weeks of blooming in the spring. I gently press the ashes into the now damp soil. It's a simple task, hands on the earth, but it feels somehow like I am putting things right.

'Ashes to ashes.'

I stand up and start to take off my gloves, brush some of the ash and soil from my gloves and garden gear into the lawn.

> *I ask just one gift from you*
> *There's no merit, it is true,*
> *Yet, consider this one plea,*
> *Will you just remember me?*

I'm a priest but I have to confess, some days I don't know if there is a God. I'm not sure that if there is a Heaven there would be much room for me. I'm on leave from my calling to minister to a flock that wants answers, and I should have all the answers to these questions about God. However, I need time to think, pray and wonder about these things. Maybe I will find an answer for me, but it won't be one I ought to share or want to share with anyone.

I go through the gate to the little cemetery at my first church in the countryside, an hour's train ride away. I never thought I would make this journey. I walk quietly to the spot where Waldo is buried beneath a simple crucifix with dancing angels circling the cross. It was a gift from a parishioner who had been doing charity work in Ethiopia. Peter insisted it be the only marking at the grave. Dancing angels? Maybe they have offered Waldo a bit of joy in this bleak spot.

I take the last of Peter's ashes and spread them carefully over Waldo's grave.

'Dust to dust.'

*

A swarm of youngsters selling everything from chewing gum to lottery cards, bananas to sunhats, greet me along with the oven-like heat as I exit the Norman Manley International Airport in Kingston, Jamaica. How will I ever find Sophia? Taxis honking, minibuses jockeying for position, great long coaches offloading or loading tourists from the United States, Canada and Great Britain.

But there she is, her head wrapped in gold and her now much thinner body garbed in purple. She is at home.

Sophia called three weeks ago on her new phone, confirming my visit. The congregation is without a minister because they have no money, as unemployment is high, and she asked me on the phone if I might take the services for a couple of months.

I told her I would think about it while on the plane, saying, 'I don't know how much help I would be, Sophia. I don't know really what I believe any more. Though I haven't totally given up hope.'

'That's good,' she said. 'That's just what we need.'

As she drives along the winding country road to her village, I know she wants to ask me about taking the services. I want to ask her about Charles. We talk about everything else. I update her on Josh and Derek, Tom and Francis, the congregations. She finds her opening.

'Have you been thinking about helping our little church, Faith? You said you hadn't given up hope?'

'You remember my very words.'

'Of course, Faith. I listen closely to you.'

We laugh.

'I haven't given up hope but ... I'm just not sure.'

We turn a sharp corner and head towards an old wooden church, painted bright blue with a massive cross outside. Beneath the cross is a sign painted in large black and white letters.

'See,' she says. 'Hope Church! What a place to find out if there is any hope.'

Sophia laughs at her joke.

I just stare at the sign, the church.

'What do you think, Faith? Isn't it time, time for a new beginning?'

I look at Sophia's broad smile, take a deep breath.

'Yes,' I say.

Final Words

New voices ...
faint
then
no longer muffled
behind thin masks
of disbelief.
Angry,
apocalyptic,
crying out
amid
perilous winds
that batter homes,
families,
businesses,
hospitals,
shelters –
huddled together
in
villages,
sharing stories
that may save us
even as
we are
locked down –
'Isolate,
'Stay safe.
'Create.'
It's the new way,
of being
community.

Acknowledgements

I have been blessed over the past three years of writing these stories with a community of literary support that included early readers – Jeffrey Warren, Michael Sargent, Brian Clover, James Hill, Dean Salter, Ian Robertson, Ian Morton-Wright, Ewan Hooper, William MacKinnon, Christina Paradela and Patricia Hughes.

It has been a privilege and pleasure to have been mentored during this period by the wonderfully wise Katherine Stansfield, who has helped shape these stories, pointing towards the 'Areas Requiring Attention'. Tim Major's sharp editor's eye aided in the precision of the language, and by making the text more readable.

My partner, Patricia Hughes, continued to provide moral support and cups of tea, even while being asked to read 'that paragraph' for the umpteenth time. Claire Asling and Martin Asling allowed Dad to bang on about writing stories ad nauseum in those lovely long-distance phone calls.

To all, thank you. I am most grateful.

The story 'Too Old for Scandal' originated in a conversation I had with Rod Morrison at our local a year before he died. He was a great reader and storyteller, so I am disappointed he did not get to read the story he inspired. Rest in peace.

This collection is dedicated to the memory of my mother, Viola Asling (Godman), who knew something about lost children. She died in 1998. I still talk to her every day.

'A Time for Every Matter' first appeared in *Sentinel Literary Quarterly*.

'Death of a Pacifist' first appeared on the *LitroUSA* website.

Any errors belong to me alone.

John P. Asling

Lightning Source UK Ltd.
Milton Keynes UK
UKHW040643150920
369944UK00001B/205